Between Us

BENITO RICARDO

Between Us
Copyright © 2022 by Benito Ricardo

Ordering Information:
Quantity sales: special discounts are available on quantity purchases by corporations, associations, and others. For details, contact the publisher at the address below.

Publisher's Cataloging-in-Publication data
Heyliger, Benito R. Between Us

The main category of the book — Fiction / Erotica / Gay www.austinmacauley.com/us
First Published (2019)
Austin Macauley Publishers LLC 40 Wall Street, 28th Floor
New York, NY 10005 USA

mail-usa@austinmacauley.com
+1 (646) 5125767

ISBN
978-1-957378-05-3 (Paperback)
978-1-957378-04-6 (eBook)

Benito R. Heyliger is also the author of other romance books, including *First Kiss* and *The Chapel Wedding*. Though he lives in Charleston, South Carolina, with his cat and dog, he loves to travel, and has been to six continents except Antarctica.

This romance novel, *Between Us,* is dedicated to my parents, George and Maude Heyliger, who have taught me the various aspects of life since I was a small child. I can never thank them enough for all the support, encouragement, and for teaching me the value of education in the current world. I will forever be grateful and I am truly blessed to have them in my life.

Table of Contents

Chapter One

Samuel was sitting at one of the tables by himself, playing with the drink in front of him, when a blond guy with a cheeky grin, about the same height as Samuel, approached him. Samuel recognized him as Julius' best man. He had been invited to Benjamin and Julius' wedding, but didn't really know anyone except the happy couple. So, after dinner, he ended up alone at the table when everyone just seemed to disappear.

"Hi, I'm Kyle." Kyle introduced himself as he sat down next to Samuel, placing his nearly empty glass on the table. Samuel could tell that he'd already had a few drinks although he wasn't drunk yet.

"Samuel."

"So, how do you know Julius and Ben?" When Samuel looked up, he was surprised to see Kyle watching him intently while waiting for him to answer.

"I went to college with Ben and we became friends."

"Cool. I'm best friends with Julius. So, how come I've never seen you before?"

"I figured that with you being his best man. If I meet up with them, it's usually only the three of us. I'm not that good at dealing with too many people, never mind strangers."

"You're doing fine with me. But I can go if you'd rather be on your own." Samuel didn't fail to notice the disappointment that crossed Kyle's face for a few seconds before it was replaced by understanding.

"It's okay, you're welcome to stay." Samuel gave Kyle a soft smile as he was still looking at him.

"Thanks." Kyle grinned back at him, and just as he was about to say something else, another guy approached them.

"Kyle, come and join us over at the other table," the guy said and Samuel was sure that would be the end of his conversation with Kyle.

"I'm good here, thanks. Danny, this is Samuel, he's one of Ben's friends. Samuel, this is Daniel."

Samuel was surprised Kyle had chosen to stay with him, even though he shouldn't have been when he remembered Kyle's disappointed look a few minutes earlier. And he was being introduced to his friends, so it took a few seconds longer to greet the guy.

Samuel and Kyle ended up talking to each other all evening, with a few more interruptions by Kyle's friends. They tried to get him back to their table, but Kyle wouldn't leave Samuel's side. Samuel found that Kyle was still staring at him, as if he was really intrigued by him, when Ben and Julius wandered up to them.

"Having fun, Kyle?" Julius asked cheerily, clearly tipsy already, as he sat down next to Kyle and slung his arm over his shoulders.

"I'm definitely having fun. This has been a great wedding," Kyle answered as he turned his head to look at Julius.

"Whoa, you're still sober?"

"I wouldn't say I'm sober. I did have a couple of drinks."

"Usually, you'd be drunk by now. Are you sure you're having fun?"

"Oh my God, you're making me sound like an alcoholic. Yes I am. I'm just getting to know Samuel a bit better."

When Julius saw Benjamin quietly talking to Samuel, he knew he had to take his chance to talk to Kyle about Samuel. Even though he was Ben's friend, Julius was fond of him and he appreciated Samuel always being there for them. "Come and get a fresh round of drinks with me, Kyle?"

Kyle was about to protest, but when he took a look at Julius' serious face, he knew he wanted to talk to him alone. "Sure."

As soon as they had asked Samuel and Benjamin if they wanted another drink, they made their way to the bar. But before they could reach it, Julius pulled Kyle aside.

"Why have you never introduced me to Samuel?" Kyle inquired, before Julius was even able to say anything.

Julius sighed softly as he ran a hand through his hair. "Samuel is not good with strangers. It took him ages to warm up to me, and he prefers it when there aren't too many people around."

"He's doing fine with me. Although, he's really, really quiet."

"It seems so, which is a real surprise." When Julius and Benjamin had watched Kyle and Samuel chatting to each other before coming over, they were genuinely surprised to see that Samuel had warmed up to Kyle so quickly. "And that will change when he knows you better. But Kyle, please don't play with him."

"What? I've never played with anyone and you know that!"

"I'm sorry, I didn't mean it like that." Julius exhaled heavily as he looked at Kyle apologetically before continuing, "Are you really interested in him?"

"What kind of question is that? Of course, he intrigues me and I'd like to get to know him better."

"Fair enough. But I have to warn you, he's not a one-night stand kind of guy. If that's all you're looking for then you need to leave him alone."

"I'm not looking for a one-night stand," Kyle reassured Julius as he wondered what Samuel's story was. "Did anything happen to him?"

"I can't tell you that. I can only tell you that you need to be patient with him and give him time and space, then you might be one of the lucky ones he actually lets in. I promise you it will be worth it when he does. Samuel is a great guy and an awesome friend."

After their little chat, they finally got the drinks and made their way back to the table where they found Samuel and Ben in a deep conversation. Kyle admired how openly Samuel was talking to Ben and, in that moment, he vowed to himself that he would give Samuel all the time in the world. He hoped to get to know him so well that he would be talking to Kyle just as freely.

Julius and Benjamin stayed just a little longer with them before they disappeared to attend to their other guests as well, leaving Kyle and Samuel on their own again until another guy came over to persuade Kyle away from Samuel.

"You don't have to stay with me, Kyle. You can go and spend time with your friends if you want." Samuel told him quietly. He felt bad for monopolizing so much of Kyle's time, although he guessed that Kyle didn't mind spending time with him by the way he was still looking at him.

"Nope, I'm good here. Unless you want me to leave you alone." Kyle grinned happily at Samuel when he shook his head. Samuel felt all warm inside, experiencing a feeling he wasn't really used to.

Everyone had gathered around in the function room of the hotel where the reception was held to send Julius and Ben off onto their wedding night. When they'd gone, Samuel told Kyle that he was heading back up to his room as well, thanking him for spending the evening with him.

"Can I have your number?" Kyle asked just as Samuel had turned around and was about to walk away. This caused Samuel to whirl around in astonishment, staring at Kyle for a few seconds.

"You want my number?" Samuel's mind was reeling; he still wasn't sure what to make of Kyle's obvious interest in him. At first, he had thought Ben and Julius had asked Kyle to entertain him, but he could see the interest was real. He had asked Ben, who had denied it straight away and told him that it's impossible to make Kyle do anything he didn't want to do.

"Yes, please, if you don't mind. I'd really like to get to know you better."

"I…" Samuel was perplexed that Kyle actually wanted to see him again. But just as he was going to answer, he got interrupted by two of Kyle's friends.

"Kyle!" The guy Kyle had introduced as Daniel earlier nearly shouted as he threw his arm around Kyle's shoulder and pulled him closer, clearly drunk already. "Are you finally done being all nice to this guy?"

Kyle turned his head to glare at Danny. When he turned back to apologize to Samuel, he saw that he had disappeared. "Thanks, Danny," Kyle said sarcastically before turning to a sorry-looking Carlos. "Take care of him, okay? I need to go after Samuel."

"I will and I'm sorry, Kyle," Carlos apologized and Kyle nodded his acceptance before he rushed after Samuel.

"Samuel, wait!" Kyle called out just as Samuel was stepping into the lift even though he wasn't sure if he would after what Danny had said. But to his delight, Samuel stopped the door from closing and waited for Kyle to get in. "Thank you. I'm so sorry about Danny; he's just drunk and doesn't mean any harm."

"It's okay. He's right though, you barely spent any time with your friends because of me."

"I wanted to spend time with you, you have to believe me." Kyle wasn't above begging, he was desperate to make sure Samuel believed him and he still had a chance to get to know him.

"I do believe you."

"Really?"

The surprise was clear on Kyle's face and Samuel gave him a soft smile. "Really. Ben said that you didn't do anything unless you wanted to and I trust him. I've also kind of seen it myself when your friends tried to make you join them and you chose to stay with me."

"I never do anything I don't want to." Kyle winked cheekily as the lift came to a stop and they got out on Samuel's floor. Kyle followed Samuel to his room. "So, can I have your number?"

Samuel turned to look at Kyle when he had unlocked his door. As he studied Kyle's genuine expression, he felt an overwhelming urge to invite him into his room, "Sure. Want to come in?" Just as he asked that, he realized how it might sound to Kyle so he hurried to add, "Uh, to talk, you know."

The giant grin that appeared on Kyle's face should have been answer enough for Samuel, yet he still needed to hear it from Kyle before fully opening the door and letting them in.

"I'd love to." Samuel marveled at how genuinely happy Kyle seemed to be about this until he felt his hand on his arm, squeezing gently. Samuel looked down at it, causing Kyle to withdraw his hand immediately. "Sorry, I didn't mean to overstep…"

"It's fine," Samuel interrupted him as he finally opened the door fully and signaled for Kyle to go in.

Kyle and Samuel spent the next hour chatting in Samuel's room until Kyle noticed that Samuel could barely keep his eyes open anymore and decided to leave him in peace.

"I should go and let you get some sleep, you look tired." Kyle was reluctant to leave, but when Samuel yawned, he knew it was the right thing to do.

"Yeah, sorry, I had a short night." Samuel would have loved to spend more time with Kyle, but he really was tired. It wasn't until he noticed Kyle's perplexed look that he realized what Kyle must be thinking after what he just said. Although, it was pretty clear that he did not have a significant other in his life; at least in his own eyes. "I was working late."

"Oh, right." Kyle sounded so relieved and Samuel felt all warm inside. "What do you do?"

"I'm a software engineer." Samuel mentally braced himself, waiting for the comments that usually followed when he told people what his profession was. But they never came. Instead, Kyle looked rather impressed.

"Wow, you must be really smart."

"Not really," Samuel shrugged his shoulders, dismissing what Kyle had said.

"You develop software?" Kyle asked, and when Samuel nodded, he continued, "Then you are really smart. I can't even figure out why my laptop is being all slow." Kyle joked about his own cluelessness when it came to computers while Samuel blushed at the compliment.

"I'm just really interested in computers. I can have a look at your laptop if you want." Samuel offered when he realized that Kyle might have some problems with his laptop.

"Oh, you don't have to. That's not why I said it."

"I know. The offer still stands though."

"That would be great, thanks. I'll pay you, of course." Kyle didn't want Samuel thinking he was going to take advantage of him, but Samuel just told him it was no problem and that it wasn't necessary for Kyle to pay him.

When Samuel yawned again, Kyle nearly slapped his hand against his forehead, remembering that he wanted to leave so Samuel could get some sleep.

"Sorry for keeping you up. You should have just kicked me out. I'll go now. But before I go, will you finally give me your number?" Kyle smiled at Samuel angelically as he handed him his phone so he could put his number in.

"It's no problem," Samuel said as he typed in his number before giving the phone back to Kyle. Even though he was dead tired, he still enjoyed spending time with Kyle. "Thank you for spending your time with me tonight."

"It was my pleasure. I'll definitely get in touch with you in the next couple of days, if that's okay with you."

"Sure."

"Cool. Right, I better go." Both of them got up and made their way to the door where Kyle turned to face Samuel again. He nearly went in for a hug when he thought better of it, not being sure if Samuel liked physical contact. "Can I hug you?"

When Samuel nodded dazedly, Kyle went in for a short hug, not wanting to overwhelm him or make him uncomfortable, before saying his final goodbye for that night, leaving Samuel to get some sleep.

Just as Samuel had gotten into bed, his phone vibrated with an incoming message. As he checked it, he saw it was from an unknown number.

Sweet dreams… Kyle

When Julius and Benjamin had reached the honeymoon suite and closed the door behind them, Benjamin turned to Julius.

"Did you set Kyle up to spend time with Samuel?"

"No. Even if I had tried, you should know that Kyle doesn't do anything unless he wants to."

Julius looked confused as Ben burst into laughter, trying to calm down so he could talk. "I said the same when Samuel asked me. Have you spoken to Kyle about him?"

"Yes, I told him a bit about Samuel, but not too much. I don't want to betray Samuel's trust in me." Benjamin smiled softly at that. "Kyle seems to be really interested in him though. Maybe we should have introduced them to each other sooner."

"No, it's perfect this way. Kyle's own initiative will show Samuel that he can trust him. I think he already does, a tiny bit at least."

Chapter Two

It was two days after the wedding when Samuel received another message from Kyle. They ended up messaging for a while until Kyle asked if Samuel would like to watch a movie with him on Saturday. Samuel thought about it for a couple of minutes until he replied that they could watch it at Samuel's home and for Kyle to bring his laptop so he could have a look at it then.

It was late Saturday afternoon when Kyle was stood in front of Samuel's house, nervously waiting for him to open the door. He wasn't one to be nervous, but he wasn't entirely sure if Samuel was still up for this. He did rationalize that Samuel would have cancelled if he wasn't. They had exchanged a few more messages but on Thursday, Kyle only got a short text telling him that Samuel was really busy with work. Since then, he hadn't heard from him again.

When the door was finally opened, it wasn't Samuel who stood in front of him though, but a really tall, dark-haired guy who looked at Kyle curiously. Kyle wondered if he had the right address.

"Hi, does Samuel live here?"

"Yes."

"I'm Kyle. Samuel invited me over for today."

"Oh, right, you're the guy he spent time with at the wedding. Come in." The guy opened the door wide and let Kyle in, facing him when he had closed the door, finally introducing himself, "I'm Alex. Samuel's just in the shower, but he shouldn't be too much longer."

After Kyle had taken his shoes off, Alex showed him into the living room and then offered him a drink as Kyle sat down on the couch. He wondered why Samuel hadn't told him he had a partner as he was certain that his interest in Samuel had been obvious, and why he hadn't brought him to the wedding. Just as Alex had returned with his drink, they heard the shower shut off and then Alex yelled out loudly, "Samuel, come down here for a second."

It didn't take long until Samuel was stood in the doorway in a fluffy bathrobe. He blushed when he realized Kyle was sat in his living room.

"Oh God, I'm so sorry. I forgot that I invited you over. Work was really busy the last two days and I haven't had much sleep."

"It's okay, I understand. I can just go home again."

"No. I want you to stay," Samuel told him just as he was about to get up. For the first time since they had known each other, it was Kyle who looked astonished as he met Samuel's eye, who smiled at him softly. "I'll just get dressed, I won't be long."

Alex excused himself nearly straight away after Samuel had disappeared and followed him to his bedroom, drumming his fingers on the door softly so Kyle wouldn't hear it. It took a few seconds until Samuel opened his door in just his boxers with a pair of jeans in his hand and a confused look on his face. Alex ignored the look and made his way into Samuel's bedroom, pushing him away from the door before closing it.

"Kyle thinks I'm your boyfriend."

"What? Has he said that?"

"No, you just have to watch him, it's obvious. I'll show you when we get back to him."

"Alex…"

"What? I'll even let you put him out of his misery by telling me to get lost." Alex winked at Samuel, being extremely proud of his plan. "He really likes you. He looks at you like you're special to him."

"I know," Samuel confessed quietly, a soft blush spreading over his cheeks, and then continued when he saw the perplexed look on Alex's face, "What? I'm not blind."

"Then go for it."

"I don't…"

"Samuel, he's Julius' best friend so I can't imagine him to be a bad guy."

"Yeah, from what I've seen so far he's a really nice guy."

"There you go; you're starting to trust him already. Now get dressed, I'll go back to him."

"Would you actually get me a coffee instead?"

When Alex had left after nodding, Samuel finally got dressed and then made his way back to Kyle in the living room, apologizing for the delay.

"It's fine. Are you sure you don't want me to leave?"

"Absolutely," Samuel smiled at Kyle as he got comfortable on the couch before Alex came back with a cup of coffee for Samuel. "Thanks, Alex."

When Samuel had safely deposited the cup on the table, Alex bent down from where he was perching on the arm of the couch and pulled Samuel into a half hug, kissing his cheek. "You're welcome."

"Argh, Alex, get lost. Go home, I'm sure your boyfriend will appreciate it."

"Mike is actually at work, but since I'm not wanted here I'll go home anyway." Alex sounded hurt when he said that, and for a moment, Kyle felt extremely guilty. But then he saw Alex sticking his tongue out at Samuel, who laughed softly at that. It was only then that Kyle realized that Samuel and Alex were not together now that he knew Alex was with someone else. Kyle breathed a silent sigh of relief, thinking to himself that he might still have a chance with Samuel.

When Alex had left, Kyle turned to Samuel as he told him about his worries that he had interrupted them and felt guilty that Alex was the one who had to leave.

"It's fine, we hadn't made any plans. Alex usually just shows up when he knows I'm home because I'll just forget when I'm not getting enough sleep," Samuel shrugged his shoulders as he sipped on his coffee. "Did you bring your laptop?"

"Uh yeah, but you don't have to look at it if you're tired."

"I'm fine. You can pick a movie while I have a look at it," Samuel said before he pointed to a huge cabinet with DVDs in it, confident that it would keep Kyle busy for a little while as he worked on his laptop.

Kyle was impressed with the amount of DVDs Samuel owned and told him so before he scurried off to fetch his laptop, which he then handed over to Samuel. Samuel then proceeded to turn on the laptop straight away, asking Kyle if it was password protected, to which he just shook his head while making his way over to the cabinet.

While Samuel waited for the laptop to boot, he watched Kyle looking at his DVDs in awe, not knowing where to start first. Samuel told him they were arranged alphabetically, which gifted him a lovely smile from Kyle.

Samuel continued to watch Kyle with an absentminded smile on his face as his thoughts drifted off. Should he listen to Alex and take his chance with Kyle? Kyle was clearly interested in him and Alex had been right when he said that Kyle thought they were a couple. He could clearly see the disappointment on Kyle's face when Alex had kissed his cheek, which turned into relief as soon as he realized they weren't together. Alex had another point as well—he couldn't imagine Kyle to be a bad guy or that he was just interested in him so he could gain something. Samuel was sure he wouldn't have been Julius' best friend if he was and he could see that Kyle was genuinely interested in him. His decision was made as he remembered the way Kyle had looked at him at the wedding. As that same warm feeling that he'd experienced that night enveloped him again, Samuel knew he was going to give Kyle a chance.

Samuel worked away quietly on the laptop until he realized he'd have to make a few changes, but when he looked up to ask Kyle for permission, he saw him looking at the DVDs with one hand hovering near one of them, unsure if he was allowed to remove it. Samuel told him to pick out any DVD he liked and that they could narrow it down later or Kyle could borrow them if he wanted before asking him to come over. As soon as Kyle had sat down next to him, Samuel asked him a lot of questions before he proceeded to ask Kyle's permission to change a few things, which he was given immediately.

After another while of trying out different things Samuel sighed in frustration, knowing that he'd have to clear the laptop completely to see where the problem was. He wasn't sure Kyle was going to like that.

"Are you okay?" Kyle asked as he heard Samuel sigh, pulling him out of his thoughts. Samuel could see the worry on Kyle's face.

"Yeah, I'm fine. I just can't fix your laptop without deleting and then reinstalling Windows."

"Oh, alright; well, thank you for trying anyway."

"No, I wasn't telling you that I'm giving up. Is it okay if I save all your data and then continue?"

"Uh sure. But you really don't have to do this if it's taking too long."

"It's no problem. I'll just set this up in my office. I won't be long. Or you can join me."

"I'm good here, thanks. I've got a few more DVDs to look through."

When Samuel returned from his office, Kyle was just picking out the last DVD he liked and put it onto the pile he had made on top of the cabinet.

"Are you hungry, Kyle? I know it's a bit early, but I'm starving." When Samuel's stomach had grumbled, he realized how hungry he actually was, which was no surprise as he had been sleeping until he had got woken up by Alex earlier.

"Sure, I could eat."

"Right, so what do you want? Chinese, pizza, or something else?"

"I'm not too fussy. Pick whatever you'd like."

"Pizza?" Samuel asked hopefully and Kyle nodded immediately, both of them agreeing on the toppings before Samuel ordered their food.

The doorbell rang about half an hour later, just as Samuel had excused himself to go to the bathroom. Kyle called out that he'd get it instead, Samuel having told him that the money for it was lying on the little table in the entrance hall before he left. But Kyle ignored Samuel's money and took out his own cash to pay for their food. He made his way into the kitchen and set the food down on the counter just as Samuel returned.

"Thanks for getting the door. Would you like something to drink? I have beer, juice, water…"

"Water is fine. I still have to drive home."

"Oh, you don't live nearby?"

"No, well, not in walking distance anyway."

"You could have one beer. I mean, we're still going to watch a movie so you'll be here for a little while longer and you should be okay to drive home later."

"True. Yeah, okay, I'll have a beer too."

Samuel took two bottles of beer out of the fridge and handed them to Kyle before he grabbed their food. Both of them made their way into the living room, where Samuel set the food down on the couch table. He told Kyle to make himself comfortable on the couch before he went and got the pile of DVDs Kyle had picked out earlier. He asked him if there was one in particular that Kyle wanted to watch. When Kyle pointed to one of them, Samuel put it on straight away— both of them watching while they ate their food.

"Do you want another beer?" Samuel asked when Kyle had put down his empty bottle.

"No, I'm driving, remember?"

"Well, you could stay here," Samuel offered and then continued as Kyle stared at him in shock, "If you want to. I have guest rooms. And I won't have your laptop finished until tomorrow either."

"Are you sure? You barely know me," Kyle honestly hadn't expected Samuel to offer for him to stay the night. He could tell that Samuel had started to trust him already and it reflected in his actions as well.

"That might be true, but we're changing that, aren't we? And you being Julius' best friend helps as well. He trusts you and I don't see why I shouldn't trust you. So yes, I'm absolutely sure."

"Okay, then I'd love to stay. I'd also like another beer, but I can get that myself." Kyle had gotten up and scurried into the kitchen so fast that Samuel didn't have any time to react until Kyle reappeared with two bottles of beer. He handed him one.

It was just approaching 9 p.m. when the movie they were watching finished. Samuel stretched himself before he turned to face Kyle, who was already looking at him.

"Do you want to watch another movie? It's a bit early for bed."

"We don't have to. We could talk for a while, if you're up for it?"

"I know I'm quiet, but I do like talking to my friends. And I really enjoy talking to you." Samuel chuckled softly when he saw Kyle's stunned expression. He realized that Samuel had just admitted that he counted Kyle as a friend already. "I just need to check on the progress of your laptop first. And I also need to put fresh sheets on your bed."

"I can help with that. Well, I can put fresh sheets on my bed. I wouldn't be much help with the laptop."

Samuel told him that he didn't have to help, but Kyle insisted on it. While Samuel checked on the laptop after he had shown Kyle to the guest room and provided him with fresh sheets, Kyle made his bed. He then wandered into Samuel's office when he was done before both of them returned to the living room.

When it had just gone past 11 p.m. and they had talked for nearly two hours, Kyle suggested that they should head off to bed. Samuel kept yawning and he did look tired as well. Samuel, feeling guilty about it, tried to downplay his tiredness, but Kyle was having none of that. He was adamant to make certain that they went to bed so Samuel could catch up on his sleep.

Samuel accompanied Kyle to his room, and when they had reached the door, he inquired if Kyle needed any clothes to sleep in. Kyle just shook his head and said he always slept in his boxers anyway. Kyle told him that he was fine and didn't need anything else before saying goodnight to Samuel and disappearing into his room.

Samuel was in his office when he heard Kyle coming down the next morning and gently knocking on the open door.

"Morning," Kyle's voice sounded rough, and when Samuel turned around to look at him, he could clearly see how tired Kyle still was. Kyle stood in the doorway in just his t- shirt and boxers and his hair looked a mess, constantly falling into his face. Samuel's heart skipped a beat at the sight in front of him. Samuel knew at that moment that he was falling for Kyle.

"Good morning. Did you not sleep well?" Samuel wasn't sure if Kyle looked like that every morning or if he really hadn't slept well.

"I slept fine once I actually fell asleep. It was just too hot," Kyle replied as he took in the sight of Samuel wearing a vest and some sweatpants, sitting in front of his own computer and Kyle's laptop. He was still working away at it with a cup of coffee next to him. "Please tell me you didn't stay up all night to fix my laptop."

"No, I didn't. I got up about an hour ago and I just finished reinstalling Windows. It's running a lot faster now. I only have to move your data back onto it and install your programs again. But that can wait for now. Would you like some breakfast?"

"Uh…" Kyle tiredly rubbed his eyes as he tried to process what Samuel had just told him.

"Do you want to go back to bed and sleep a bit more?"

"No, that would be rude. I'm sorry; I just need to wake up properly. Would it be okay if I took a shower?"

"Of course. Come on, I'll get you some towels and you can use the shower in my en-suite." Samuel got up and then showed Kyle to his bedroom after a little detour to pick up some towels for him.

"Could I borrow some boxer shorts and a t-shirt from you?"

"Sure," Samuel retrieved both items for Kyle, handing them to him. Then he disappeared in his en-suite, rummaging around in one of the cabinets before he came back out with a new toothbrush in his hand. "Feel free to use whatever you need. If there's something you can't find, just look through the cabinets. Although, I don't have anything you can style your hair with, sorry."

"Thank you. I'm sure I'll survive a day without styling my hair," Kyle winked as he grinned at Samuel, who was glad to see that Kyle's cheeky self had made an appearance again. He gave Kyle a soft smile in return and then inquired what Kyle would like for breakfast. He told him that he wasn't fussy and cereal or toast would do, but that he would like some coffee.

Once Samuel had left, Kyle jumped into the shower and instantly felt more awake as the cool water hit his skin. When he was finished, he dried himself off and got dressed in the boxers and t-shirt that Samuel had given him. He brushed his teeth afterwards, and then made his way to the kitchen.

He could hear the radio playing softly before he even reached the door. When he realized that Samuel hadn't heard him approaching, he stopped in the doorway to take in the sight of him. He stood at the oven cooking breakfast, and he now properly appreciated his wearing a vest that showed off his broad back and muscles.

Samuel was almost done making breakfast when he felt like he was being watched. As he turned around, he caught Kyle, who looked so much more awake after his shower, looking at him intently before Kyle became aware that he was staring.

"It smells delicious. Can I help with anything?"

"Nope, you have perfect timing. It's all done." Samuel had just turned off the stove as he put the last items on their plates. He then handed them to Kyle, telling him to sit down, while Samuel got them both a cup of coffee.

When they were finished with breakfast, they both cleared everything away. Samuel turned to Kyle after he had closed the door of the dishwasher, just about to tell him that he'd finish his laptop when Kyle spoke before he could.

"Will you go out to dinner with me on Friday? As a date?" Kyle asked, but regretted it straight away when he saw Samuel's shocked face and him not giving any response. But when he was about to tell Samuel that it was okay if he didn't want to, a heart-warming smile appeared on Samuel's face. Kyle relaxed slightly.

"I'd love to. But could we change it to Saturday?" It wasn't that Samuel had plans for Friday, but with Friday being one of his regular work days, he feared he'd have to work overtime. He just wanted to make sure that he would be on time for their date and that he had enough time to get ready.

"Of course. I'll make a reservation and then let you know what time I'm picking you up at." Kyle was so relieved that Samuel hadn't rejected him. He grinned happily at Samuel as he asked, "Can I hug you?"

When Samuel had given his approval, Kyle went in for a hug, intending to keep it as short as the one on the night they had met because he didn't want to overwhelm Samuel. But just as he was about to let go again, he felt Samuel's arms wrapping around his waist, holding him close.

"You're very affectionate, aren't you?" Samuel asked when both of them had pulled out of the hug.

"Uh-huh."

"I bet that went down well with Ben," Samuel chuckled softly at his own joke and then watched as Kyle burst out laughing at the memory.

Kyle told Samuel how he had always hugged Julius. When he met Benjamin for the first time, he went in for a hug out of habit, ending in a rather awkward hug with Ben standing stock-still and Kyle pulling back immediately. Samuel laughed wholeheartedly at the description while Kyle realized that that was the first time he heard Samuel laugh properly. He decided he liked the sound of Samuel's laugh. "He's fine with me hugging him now."

"Is that why you always ask permission to hug me?" When Kyle had nodded, Samuel continued, "You don't have to ask me. If you want to hug me, just do it."

When Samuel was finished with Kyle's laptop, Kyle decided it was time to leave Samuel in peace, not wanting to outstay his welcome. He told Samuel he would be heading home now. After thanking Samuel for fixing his laptop, Kyle inquired what he owed Samuel, who still insisted that Kyle didn't have to pay him. He refused any money Kyle tried to give him, jokingly stating that Ben and Julius would be mad at him if he did. Samuel assured Kyle that it was no big deal for him to fix it and that he never charged his friends unless there were new parts involved.

After rolling his eyes in defeat, Kyle accepted it and both of them made their way to the front door. Kyle put on his shoes just as Samuel discovered that the money for the pizza was still lying on the little table.

"Kyle!"

"What?" Kyle was confused when he looked up at Samuel, but soon understood his reaction when he saw what Samuel was pointing at.

"That's your money."

"You don't want my money for fixing my laptop so I'm not taking your money for the food either."

"You were never supposed to pay for the food."

"Tough luck," Kyle smirked at Samuel before drawing him into another hug. "Thanks for a lovely time. I look forward to Saturday." When Kyle pulled back from the hug, he placed a chaste kiss on Samuel's cheek. He then let go of him completely before saying goodbye, leaving a stunned Samuel behind.

Chapter Three

It was late Saturday afternoon as Samuel tried to get ready for his date with Kyle. He had just finished his shower and put on some sweatpants and a t-shirt when his doorbell rang. Samuel frowned in confusion, he wasn't expecting anyone and it was too early to be Kyle. He would only pick him up in about an hour. Still, Samuel made his way to the front door, pulling it open and groaning when Alex and Mike grinned at him.

"What are you two doing here?" Samuel asked, not expecting an answer as he rolled his eyes at them. He knew perfectly well why they were here and he regretted telling Alex about his date.

"What do you think? We're here to help you get ready." Alex hugged him tight before making his way into Samuel's house, ignoring Samuel's unimpressed expression. Mike was more reluctant, but as soon as Samuel nodded at him, he gave Samuel a short hug as well before following Alex into the house.

By the time Samuel had closed the door, Alex came out of his kitchen with a drink in his hand while handing another one to Mike. He grinned at Samuel.

"I really don't have time to deal with you two. I need to get ready and I need to shave as well."

"Nope, you're definitely not going to shave."

"I haven't shaved since yesterday morning, Alex."

"Exactly! You look sexy with a bit of stubble. Believe me, Kyle will love it."

"Are you sure?"

"Yes! I swear, he seems to adore you."

"Alex is right, he will love it. Can I meet him?"

"No! I want both of you gone before he arrives."

"Oh, come on, let Mike meet him. I promise we won't embarrass you or scare him away."

"Since when are you being nice to someone who's interested in me?"

"Since I actually like Kyle and he doesn't seem to be interested in you for sex or money." Alex spoke sincerely as he put his drink down and then stepped closer to Samuel. "You do know that I'm only so protective of you because I love you and only want the best for you, right?" When Samuel nodded, Alex wrapped him into a tight hug and gently kissed his temple, whispering, "I just don't want you to get hurt again."

Mike wasn't one to be left out and he joined the hug as well, wrapping his arms around both of them.

"Right, now let's get you ready for your date," Alex broke the hug and he didn't give either of them a chance to react. He grabbed Samuel's arm and pulled him to his bedroom, Mike following closely behind.

When they had finally decided on a pair of black jeans, they were trying out a few different shirts. Alex ultimately decided on a white, short sleeved button-down shirt.

"Why don't you put on a tight shirt that shows off your body?" Mike asked, wondering why Alex hadn't picked something like that. He knew Samuel owned tight shirts because he had seen him wearing them on a few occasions. Mike looked puzzled when Samuel simply told him no. Then he glanced at Alex, hoping to get an explanation of him, which he didn't get as Alex was focused on Samuel. "Why not? You definitely have a body to show off."

"So? I don't want people to like me for my body."

"I thought Kyle likes you already?"

"Kyle's definitely interested in Samuel already so he doesn't need to show off," Alex interrupted and then looked at Mike with a look that told him to drop the subject.

"So, can I meet him?"

Just as Samuel was about to answer, the doorbell rang and Samuel sighed. He had really hoped to get them out of his house before Kyle picked him up. "I guess I have no choice now."

Samuel rushed out of his bedroom and made his way downstairs, opening the door to a smiling Kyle. Kyle was dressed similar to him. He had on a pair of black jeans as well, but instead of a white button-down shirt, he wore a blue one that brought out the color of his eyes.

"Hi."

"Hi. You look lovely." Kyle admired how good Samuel looked, granted he had seen him in a suit at the wedding. Samuel looked so much more relaxed wearing casual clothes.

"So do you. Listen, Kyle…" Samuel started and then nervously licked his lips as he stepped outside and pulled the door nearly closed behind him. Kyle could feel his heart sink; was Samuel going to cancel their date? His brain was telling him that Samuel wouldn't be dressed like this if he was going to cancel. But there was something about the way that Samuel said it that made Kyle nervous. "I'm really sorry, but Alex and his boyfriend, Mike, decided to come around and help me get ready, well more like annoy me. They're still inside and Mike wants to meet you. But you don't have to if you don't want to."

"It's fine, I don't mind meeting him. And that sounds like something I would do as well so don't worry," Kyle gave Samuel a reassuring smile. He was glad that Samuel hadn't canceled their date and he was happy to meet his friends. "Are you okay with me meeting him?"

"Yes, of course. It's just that they're a little protective of me."

"That's okay, I'm sure I can handle that," Kyle grinned at Samuel and then held up the bag in his hand. "I brought back your clothes. Thanks for lending them to me."

Samuel thanked Kyle for bringing them back as he took the bag off him and then invited him in, closing the door just as Alex and Mike came down the stairs. Samuel introduced Kyle and Mike to each other and then watched on in horror as Mike grabbed Kyle's right arm. He relaxed again when he only had a closer look at Kyle's tattoos.

"Sorry, I should have asked before grabbing your arm. You've got some awesome tattoos. Do you have more?"

"It's okay. Thanks. Yeah, I have one more."

"Cool. Did you design them yourself?"

"Yes, I did. But maybe we could talk about this some other time? Samuel and I should really go, we have a dinner reservation."

They had just finished their main courses when Kyle asked if Samuel would like some dessert.

"How about we have dessert at my place? I have some cake and I'm pretty sure I have ice cream too."

"Sure, I don't mind," Kyle wasn't about to complain if he got to spend some more time with Samuel at his house. He was rather looking forward to it. Kyle asked for the bill after that, and when he had paid, Kyle drove them back to Samuel's house.

They were sitting on the couch, both enjoying their cake and coffee. Kyle moaned appreciatively every time he took a bite of the cake.

"This is fantastic. Where did you get that cake?"

"I made it myself."

"Oh, wow. It's delicious!"

"Thanks. Would you like another piece?" Samuel asked when Kyle put down his empty plate.

"I'd love another one, but I don't think I can eat anymore."

They were just chatting away while finishing their coffees when Samuel turned to Kyle. He stared at him for a few seconds before asking, "Why me? I'm sure you could have anyone; you're gorgeous."

"So are you," Kyle gently cupped Samuel's face in his hands as he said that, making sure that Samuel knew he meant that. Samuel bit his lip and Kyle wondered if he really wasn't aware of how handsome he was. "Can I kiss you?"

When Samuel had nodded, Kyle leant in slowly and softly brushed his lips against Samuel's, but was surprised at how eagerly Samuel responded to the kiss. Kyle could feel Samuel's tongue against his lips and granted him the access he was looking for. He gasped in surprise when he discovered Samuel's tongue piercing as their tongues played with each other.

"You have a tongue piercing?" Kyle asked when he broke their kiss, staring at Samuel in amazement.

"Uh-huh. Is that a problem?"

"Fuck no. That's so hot! I thought I'd seen it before, but I wasn't too sure if it was a piercing." When Samuel looked at him puzzled, he continued, "You lick your lips quite often."

"Do I?"

Kyle leant in again and breathed, "Yes, and that's hot too," against Samuel's lips before he captured them in another kiss, seeking out Samuel's tongue to play with immediately.

They spent the next couple of hours on the couch talking and kissing. Their lips were swollen from kissing so much and their hair disheveled from the other one running their hands through it. But they didn't seem to be able to stop. It was just approaching midnight when Kyle finally realized the time, and as much as he enjoyed this, he knew he should go home. He didn't want to push Samuel even though he seemed to enjoy this just as much as Kyle.

"I should go home."

"Stay?" Samuel cringed after asking that. It came out way quicker and sounding so much needier than intended, but Kyle thought Samuel regretted asking it.

"It's okay, I don't have to stay. Or I could stay in the guest room again if you do want me to stay here."

"No, I don't want you stay in the guest room."

"That's fine, I'll just head home then," Kyle was quick to reassure Samuel, not realizing that Samuel hadn't finished talking yet.

"No! Argh, Kyle, let me finish. I do want you to stay and I don't regret asking it. I just didn't like the way it came out. And you're definitely sleeping in my bed."

Kyle smiled warmly at Samuel, admiring his flushed cheeks and kiss-swollen lips as he realized he had fallen in love with Samuel already. He leant in again and rested their foreheads against each other, looking Samuel into the eye as he breathed, "I'd love to stay."

Samuel pecked Kyle on the lips quickly before pulling back completely, but still looking at Kyle as he licked his lips. "Do you want to head to bed then?"

When Kyle had nodded, both of them made their way upstairs to Samuel's bedroom and started to undress. Samuel looked on in awe as Kyle revealed a rather large chest tattoo, unbuttoning his shirt one at a time and then just letting it fall open.

"Wow, that looks amazing," Samuel reached out and gently traced the inked lines with his fingertips. He pulled back again and unbuttoned his own shirt, letting Kyle discover more piercings.

"Fuck, you have nipple piercings as well?" Kyle really hadn't expected Samuel to be into piercings. He wondered if he had another one, the piercings definitely being a turn-on for Kyle.

When they'd finally undressed to their boxers, they slipped into bed, facing each other. It wasn't long until they were back to kissing; Samuel stroking over Kyle's tattoo and Kyle gently playing with Samuel's piercings.

Once they stopped kissing, Kyle rested his forehead against Samuel's again and gazed at him. "We should probably go to sleep." Kyle knew if he didn't put a stop to it, they'd more than likely end up kissing all night. He wasn't sure if he was going to be able to hold back much longer. He definitely didn't want to pressure Samuel into anything.

"Maybe," Kyle couldn't fail to notice how disappointed Samuel sounded. He shifted them slightly so Samuel was lying on his back, placing a gentle kiss on the tip of Samuel's nose.

"We can continue this tomorrow if you want," Kyle suggested as he stroked over Samuel's toned abs, which he had admired since Samuel had taken his shirt off.

"Yeah okay."

"Good," Kyle smiled at him warmly. "How often do you work out?" Kyle was curious to know, although he was sure

Samuel must be working out nearly every day. He admired his dedication.

"I try to work out every day, but if I'm working late that's not always happening. Do you work out?"

"Yes, but not as often as you. You've got a fantastic body."

"Thanks, but so do you."

"Not as good as yours," Kyle winked and then placed a quick kiss on Samuel's lips before he settled down. He laid his head down on Samuel's chest as he slipped one of his legs between Samuel's and wrapped his arm around his waist. "Is this okay?"

"Sure," Samuel reassured him as he gently ran his fingers through Kyle's hair until Kyle had drifted off to sleep. Samuel followed closely behind.

Chapter Four

Samuel woke up the next morning, panicking slightly as he felt a heavy weight on his chest. But when he opened his eyes and saw Kyle's blond hair, all the memories from the night before came back again and he relaxed. Kyle was almost completely lying on top of him and Samuel was sure he wouldn't be able to move without waking him. He just lay there, taking it all in.

Samuel was still amazed that Kyle wanted him. He was sure that Kyle could have anyone he wanted yet he had picked Samuel. Samuel knew he was good looking, but he didn't think that was all Kyle saw in him.

Samuel was lost in his thoughts while absentmindedly playing with Kyle's hair. He didn't realize that Kyle had woken up until he felt him trail butterfly kisses over his chest.

Kyle woke up to Samuel caressing his hair and sighed contently, enjoying it for another while. He was surprised Samuel hadn't noticed that he was awake. Not wanting to startle Samuel, Kyle placed butterfly kisses on his chest and then kissed his way up to his neck. He shifted slightly as he kissed his way up to Samuel's cheek where he placed a final kiss before whispering, "Good morning."

"Morning. Did you sleep better this time?" Kyle looked relaxed and well-rested, bright-eyed even despite just having woken up. It was such a contrast to the week before.

"I slept great," Kyle smiled happily as he leant in, letting their lips meet in a soft good morning kiss.

After having breakfast in bed, they spent the rest of the morning in bed kissing and stroking skin lazily. Their lips were still swollen and their skin flushed every time they looked at each other. It was just after midday when the doorbell rang and they broke their kissing reluctantly. Samuel sighed because he knew who that would be.

"Just ignore it," Kyle whispered as he stroked Samuel's cheek.

"I'd love to, but I'm pretty sure that's Alex and Mike. Alex also has a key and he's not afraid to use it."

"Oh." Kyle looked so disappointed that their kissing session was interrupted. This prompted Samuel to lean in for another kiss, which he broke again when the doorbell rang a second time.

"You just stay here. I'll be back shortly, once I've dealt with those two idiots." Samuel jumped out of bed and put on some sweatpants before he rushed down the stairs and opened the door.

Samuel was greeted with Alex and Mike smirking at him. When Alex had a closer look at Samuel, he realized that Kyle must have stayed the night.

"You let him stay the night? Please tell me you didn't sleep with him." Alex asked and Samuel really didn't like the sound of it.

"Alex!" Mike beat him to an answer and Samuel was glad that he didn't sound impressed either.

"You better come in. I'm not discussing this with you on my doorstep." Samuel sighed as he opened the door wider to let them through and then looked at them. "I'm going to take a shower and let Kyle know that you're here. We can discuss this while Kyle's in the shower."

Samuel didn't give them a chance to say anything as he left them and made his way back upstairs to Kyle. When he opened the door to his bedroom, he found Kyle still sprawled out on his bed with his mobile in his hand, smiling broadly at whatever was on his screen. Kyle looked up at Samuel when he heard him closing the door and smiled cheekily at him.

"Come here, you have to see this." Kyle held out his free hand for Samuel, who took the few steps to the bed. He took the offered hand as he sat down, before Kyle handed him his phone. On Kyle's screen was a beautiful picture of Julius and Ben from their honeymoon. "Julius just sent this to me."

"Oh, wow, that's beautiful. They look so relaxed."

"Yeah, they sure do. Are Alex and Mike gone?" Samuel sighed softly and Kyle instantly knew they were still here. Not wanting Samuel to feel bad about it, Kyle reassured him, "It's fine. I'd better get dressed then."

"I need to talk to Alex; that's why they're still here. I'm going to take a shower and then head back downstairs. Feel free to use the shower as well. You can also stay up here a bit longer if you want."

"Do you want me to give you a bit of time with them?"

"No, feel free to come down with me or whenever you want," Samuel didn't want Kyle feeling left out. He was going to talk to Alex with or without Kyle being present.

"I'll take a shower after you and then come downstairs afterwards. Can I borrow some clothes again?"

"Sure. Just a shirt and boxer shorts again? Or do you want some sweatpants as well?"

"I'll take some sweatpants as well, if you don't mind me staying a bit longer."

"Feel free to stay as long as you'd like," Samuel smiled warmly at Kyle as he squeezed his hand.

"Not sick of me yet?" Kyle asked with a cheeky smile as he winked at Samuel.

"Hardly," Samuel leant in and placed a soft kiss against Kyle's lips before he went off. He rummaged around for some fresh clothes for both of them.

When Samuel was finished with his shower and dressed in comfy clothes, he made his way downstairs and looked for Alex and Mike. He found them in his kitchen, preparing some food.

"What are you doing?"

"We thought you and Kyle might like some lunch so we made some food for you," Mike explained when it was obvious that Alex wasn't going to provide an explanation.

"Samuel, I'm..."

"No! I'm going to talk first!" Samuel usually wasn't so direct, but he felt the need to clarify some things for Alex. "Firstly, I didn't let Kyle stay the night, I asked him to. He was going to go home. And secondly, no, I didn't sleep with him, even though that's none of your business. Kyle never made a move and he even offered to sleep in the guest room."

"I'm sorry, Samuel. I should never have said that."

"I know you are. And you're damn right you shouldn't have! It was only yesterday that you told me you liked Kyle and you've encouraged me to give him a chance since you met him. What changed?"

"Nothing. I do like him. I just jumped to conclusions and I'm sorry about that. I just can't bear to see you hurt again."

"You're an idiot, but I love you for looking out for me," Samuel smiled fondly at Alex as he stepped closer to him and pulled him into a tight hug. "You're forgiven." Samuel knew Alex needed to hear those words from him. As he felt Alex squeeze him tighter, he placed a soft kiss on his cheek.

Kyle walked into the kitchen just as Samuel and Alex pulled apart, greeting the other two as he came to a stop next to Samuel. Samuel grinned when he saw Mike looking at the ink that was poking out from under the vest he had given Kyle to wear. He had known Mike would be curious to see it.

"Is that your other tattoo?" Mike asked curiously as he still tried to see more of it.

"Huh?" Kyle was clearly confused until he realized he was only wearing a vest and there was bound to be a good bit of his tattoo on display. "Oh, yeah."

"Can I see all of it?"

Kyle looked at Samuel questioningly. He had no problem taking off his shirt in front of all of them, but he wasn't sure what Samuel would think about it.

"Don't look at me, Kyle; it's your body. If you're happy to show it then go for it, but don't let Mike pressure you into it."

"I don't mind," Kyle shrugged before he pulled the vest over his head and then let Mike and Alex have a closer look at his tattoo.

"That looks amazing! It must have taken ages."

"It took a while, yeah."

"Did it hurt?"

"Not as much as I thought it would, but then I suppose it depends on your pain tolerance. Can I put my shirt back on?"

When Mike had nodded, Kyle pulled the vest back on while Samuel suggested they eat the sandwiches Alex and Mike had prepared. He asked them if they wanted to stay for lunch as well since they had made so many. They all agreed to have the food outside on the terrace since they actually had a lovely warm summer for once. Samuel got some cold drinks out of the fridge for all of them.

"Can I help with anything?" Kyle asked. He felt weird not being able to help like Alex and Mike, but then they knew their way around Samuel's house pretty well whereas he didn't.

"Nope, we've got everything covered," Samuel smiled at Kyle and then leant in to place a gentle kiss on his lips when Kyle pouted at him. "Well, if you insist, you can carry the drinks out."

Kyle happily took the tray of drinks and followed Samuel outside where he placed the tray on the table.

"Fuck off, Mike. Alex, keep your boyfriend under control." Kyle looked on in confusion, but when Mike vacated the loveseat, he realized why Samuel had told him off.

"It was worth a try," Mike winked and then gave Samuel his cheekiest smile.

"I'm sure it was. Go sit down, Kyle," Samuel pointed to the seat Mike had vacated seconds earlier and Kyle sat down. Samuel handed out the drinks before joining Kyle on the loveseat.

They ate in relative silence and then just chatted away when they'd finished their lunch. Samuel made himself comfortable on the loveseat before putting his arm around Kyle. He pulled him closer, letting Kyle cuddle into him. He had a feeling Kyle needed a lot of physical contact and he was just too happy to provide it. He loved the feeling of Kyle being pressed up to him tightly with one of his hands lying on Samuel's thigh.

When Alex and Mike started play-fighting and then chasing each other down in the garden, Kyle cuddled into Samuel even more. He put his head onto his shoulder, Samuel placing a soft kiss on top of Kyle's head.

"I'm really sorry about those two idiots."

"You've got nothing to be sorry about. They're just being your friends," Kyle said as he pulled back a little so he could look at Samuel and then smiled at him reassuringly. Samuel knew he'd probably regret kissing Kyle while Alex and Mike could see it, but he just couldn't resist. He leant in and captured Kyle's lips in a kiss.

"God, I love your tongue piercing," Kyle groaned quietly as they broke the kiss, both of them aware that they weren't alone. He cuddled back into Samuel's side with his head on his shoulder. It didn't take long until Kyle pulled away again and looked at Samuel, who had been fidgeting since they broke their kiss, with a concerned look on his face. "Are you okay?"

"Yeah. I just need to use the bathroom."

"Why didn't you say so? I didn't mean to hold you back."

"It's not you holding me back; it's those two over there," Samuel nodded his head in the direction of Alex and Mike, who were now lying on the grass making out. When Kyle looked confused, Samuel added, "When I said they were protective of me, I really meant they're overprotective; very much so. I'm sure Alex is dying to get you on your own so he can talk to you and I bet that's what he'd do if I went to the bathroom now."

"I appreciate the concern, but I'm sure I can handle them. So off you go."

"Kyle…"

"Go! I promise you whatever they're going to say won't change the way I feel about you. You have nothing to worry about."

"You're clearly underestimating Alex. Although you might be right this time, he likes you so he probably won't do anything stupid." Samuel kissed Kyle's lips quickly before he got up, adding, "I'll be right back."

Kyle had to suppress a laugh when Alex and Mike made their way back to the table and sat down in their chairs again as soon as Samuel was inside. They looked at him with serious expressions on their faces.

"Listen, Kyle, you seem like a great guy and I can see you really like Samuel, but if you hurt him I will hunt you down and make you pay for it."

"Fair enough," Kyle had no intention of hurting Samuel. By looking at Alex's serious face, he could tell that Samuel meant an awful lot to Alex.

Alex was taken aback by Kyle not trying to reassure him that he'd never hurt Samuel, like all other guys had done. He was impressed by his willingness to take a punishment if he ever did hurt him. But when he saw a smile trying to break through on Kyle's face, he wondered if he took his warning seriously.

"Do you think this is funny?"

"No, I don't. Well, not what you said anyway. I just find it funny that Samuel was right when he told me you'd want to have a talk with me."

"Samuel knows me too well," Alex shrugged, unconcerned. "I know that he thinks I'm being overprotective, but I love him too much to see him hurt again."

"Alex!" Alex jumped slightly when he heard Samuel's voice. When Alex turned to look at Samuel, he looked unapologetic.

"I'm not sorry for looking out for you. But I am sorry for saying more than I should have; that wasn't my place."

"You bet you shouldn't have, but it's too late now anyway," Samuel sighed as he started collecting their plates, Kyle immediately helping him. Samuel was glad that Kyle just ignored what had been said.

"Any chance I could get a piece of that delicious cake?" Kyle asked with an angelic smile when all the plates and glasses were put on the tray. Samuel grinned at him broadly, glad of the distraction Kyle was providing.

"Of course. Would you like some tea or coffee with it as well?"

"I'd love a coffee, thanks. Can I help with anything?"

"Can we have some cake too?" Alex asked just as Samuel was about to answer Kyle's question. Samuel turned to Alex, glaring at him.

"I think you're pushing your luck, ace," Mike wasn't sure how much more it would take before Samuel got really annoyed with Alex and he didn't want to find out either. He could tell that Samuel really liked Kyle and wasn't impressed with Alex's interference.

"Please, Samuel?" Alex begged as he pulled a sad face.

"Fine," Samuel sighed, he knew Alex's intentions were good and he didn't see the point in holding grudges. "You can help me though."

Alex got up eagerly and grabbed the tray before making his way inside while Samuel turned back to Kyle. "Are you okay to stay out here with Mike?"

As soon as Kyle had nodded, Samuel turned to follow Alex into the house, but stopped when Kyle called out after him, "Samuel?"

"Yes?"

Turning around, Samuel was surprised to find Kyle really close to him already. He didn't stop until he was standing directly in front of Samuel, leaning into his personal space as he whispered, "Don't be too hard on Alex."

"I won't. And he knows he's been forgiven already," Samuel smiled at Kyle gently and then placed a kiss on the tip of his nose before finally heading inside.

When Samuel entered his kitchen, Alex had already started making coffee for them all. He looked up as soon as he noticed Samuel's presence.

"How mad are you at me?"

"I'm not mad at you, I'm sure you didn't do it on purpose. But Kyle didn't need to know that I've been hurt before one day after our first date. I'm just glad he ignored it, although I will tell him eventually."

"I'm sorry. I promise you this was the last time I got involved. Kyle is proving me right that he's a good guy. I really hope it works out for you this time and that Kyle is the right one." Alex wrapped Samuel into a tight hug and kissed his cheek as Samuel whispered his thanks to him.

Alex and Mike left after they'd finished their cake and coffees, leaving Samuel and Kyle to spend some more time with each other. When the door had been closed, Samuel grabbed Kyle's hand and pulled him into the living room where they got comfortable on the couch.

"Kyle, about what Alex said earlier…" Samuel started just as Kyle had cuddled into his side, but Kyle heard the unease in his voice and pulled back straight away. He cupped Samuel's face with his hands and turned his head so he was looking at him as he placed a finger against his lips.

"Shhh. You don't have to talk about it if it makes you uncomfortable. Just know that if you ever do want to talk about it, or something else for that matter, I'm here for you."

"Thank you," Samuel mumbled against Kyle's finger and then quickly kissed it before Kyle took it away again. Kyle knew Samuel wasn't just thanking him for offering his support but also for understanding that he wasn't ready to talk about it yet. So, Kyle gave him a warm smile and then leant in, brushing their lips together.

Samuel ended up putting on a movie, but neither of them was paying attention to it as they were kissing the whole time. It was late afternoon when Kyle reluctantly decided that he should head home and give Samuel some space, even though it didn't seem like he minded having Kyle around.

"I should go home," Kyle said as he stroked his thumb over Samuel's cheek and then smiled when Samuel actually pouted at him. "It's not like you won't see me again. Actually, can I take you out again on Friday or Saturday?"

"No, there's no need to take me out to see me. I'd like it better if we spent a quiet night in, if that's okay with you. I can cook dinner as well."

"Sure, that sounds great. Friday or Saturday?"

"Saturday would be better. At least then I don't have to rush dinner. But are you really going to make me wait until Saturday to see you again?"

Kyle laughed softly at Samuel's eagerness to see him again, glad that Samuel seemed to want this just as much as Kyle did. "You can see me anytime you want, just let me know when. I can come by after work or you could come to my place." When Kyle saw Samuel's apprehensive expression when he suggested he could come to Kyle's place, he knew straight away that Samuel wasn't comfortable with the idea. He added, "Your place it is then."

"I'm sorry. I just feel more comfortable in my own home."

"It's fine. It makes no difference to me. Just let me know when."

"Tomorrow? Or is that too soon?"

"Nope, that's perfect. Is it okay if I come over around seven?"

"Yeah. I'll get some takeaway for dinner for us," Samuel heaved a silent sigh of relief when Kyle agreed to seeing him again the next day. He had really been worried that it was too soon, but he couldn't wait to see Kyle again.

Kyle grinned at Samuel happily before reminding him that it was best if he went home now. Even though Samuel would have loved if he'd have stayed longer, he finally agreed to it, happy about the prospect of seeing Kyle again the next evening.

Chapter Five

It was Wednesday and Kyle was just on his lunch break when his phone rang. He was surprised to see that Samuel was calling him, answering immediately.

"Hi, Samuel. Is everything okay?"

"Hi, Kyle. Yeah, everything's fine. I was just wondering if you'd like to stay over tonight."

"I'd love to. But I need to warn you, I have to get up at 6 a.m."

"That's no problem. I'll see you tonight."

Kyle ended the call when he had said his goodbye as well, grinning happily at the thought of getting to spend more time with Samuel. He couldn't wait for work to be finished.

Kyle was on his way to Samuel's house after having a shower at his own place and picking up everything he needed so he could go straight to work from Samuel's place the next morning. He knew he was half an hour early, but Kyle was sure Samuel wouldn't mind even though he should have just gotten home himself.

When Samuel opened the door, Kyle was surprised to see him in only a pair of shorts and a baggy t-shirt. He looked sweaty and flushed, clearly having been working out. Kyle had only found out the day before that Samuel had a small gym and a swimming pool in the basement of his house.

"Hi."

"Hi, come in. Sorry, I'm all sweaty. But since I finished early, I thought I could get a workout done before you arrived. I'll just take a shower, I won't be long," Samuel explained while Kyle stepped into the house. He closed the door before turning back to Samuel, who was just turning to head upstairs to take a shower.

Kyle grabbed Samuel's wrist. When Samuel flinched and tensed up for a tiny moment before relaxing again, Kyle let go immediately. "Sorry, I didn't mean to startle you."

"It's okay, I just didn't expect your touch." Samuel smiled reassuringly at Kyle; his body language telling Kyle that he was relaxed again.

"I'm sorry for being early as well."

"Don't be, I actually love that you came over as soon as you could." Samuel gently cupped Kyle's face in his hands after he had stepped closer. "I know I'm all sweaty, but can I kiss you?"

Kyle's only answer was to lean in and capture Samuel's lips in a soft kiss.

"Have you been working out for long before I came?" Kyle asked once they broke the kiss.

"No, just about twenty minutes I'd say."

"If I can borrow some shorts and a shirt of yours, I'll join you for the workout."

"Of course you can. But you don't have to, I can just work out some other time."

"I want to and I really don't mind. I could use a workout myself."

Nodding, Samuel held out his hand for Kyle and waited until he grabbed it, intertwining their fingers, before he pulled Kyle upstairs to his bedroom. He searched for some workout clothes for Kyle while Kyle put down his back bag. By the time Samuel had found what he was looking for, Kyle had stripped out of his jeans and t-shirt. He was left in just his boxers, waiting for Samuel to hand him the clothes. Samuel waited for Kyle to slip into the clothes and then both of them made their way to the gym with a quick stop in the kitchen. Samuel grabbed a bottle of water out of the fridge for Kyle.

They worked out for about an hour before Kyle had enough and he abandoned the workout. Instead, he ended up just watching Samuel doing crunches while still sitting on the stationary bike. It didn't take long for Samuel to notice that Kyle was watching him and he gave him a lopsided grin before asking, "Had enough?"

"Yeah, I don't think I have the same stamina as you do."

"Do you want to take a shower already? I'm just going to do a few more crunches and then I'll come up as well."

"Sure," Kyle agreed. He would have loved to watch Samuel some more and then take a shower with him, but he wasn't going to push for it. Instead, he got off the bike and walked over to Samuel, crouching down in front of him and placing a kiss on his lips when he came up from a crunch. "Take your time. Do you want me to make some dinner?"

"There's food in the fridge. It just needs to be heated up in the oven for a bit."

By the time Samuel was finished with his shower and he joined Kyle in the kitchen, he found Kyle preparing a salad for them, only wearing a pair of tight fitting boxers. When he reached him, he wrapped his arms around Kyle's waist from behind and placed a soft kiss on his shoulder as Kyle relaxed into him. Kyle was glad that he hadn't put a shirt on when he felt Samuel's bare chest pressed against his back. He relaxed into Samuel's arms.

"I hope you don't mind that I made a salad as well."

"Not at all. I'd forgotten I had those ingredients anyway."

"When did you have time to make that lasagna?"

"I had that in the freezer and took it out yesterday evening. I usually cook food on the weekends and then freeze it. It's easier to just have to heat it up when I'm working."

Kyle hummed in understanding when he felt Samuel's lips on his shoulder again, slowly, teasingly, kissing his way to Kyle's neck and up to his ear. He placed a final kiss just behind his ear before pulling back completely.

After dinner, they decided on a movie, but ended up kissing the whole time. Kyle eventually straddled Samuel's lap as they explored all the skin that was on display. Samuel was being really quiet and Kyle feared he wasn't enjoying it as much as Kyle was. When he sucked on his nipples and started playing with the barbells, Samuel moaned out loud, clearly having sensitive nipples. Kyle played with them a bit longer.

It didn't take too long until Kyle could feel that Samuel was hard and he was sure Samuel could feel Kyle's hard cock as well. Samuel shuffled forward on the couch and then stood up with Kyle in his arms. Kyle squealed in surprise.

"Whoa, Samuel, put me down. I'm way too heavy."

"You're really not. Do you trust me?" Samuel asked, looking Kyle in the eye.

"Of course," Kyle answered without hesitation and then he kissed Samuel's nose quickly.

"Then just hold on to me. I promise I won't drop you."

When Kyle had nodded and wrapped his arms and legs tightly around Samuel, Samuel made his way upstairs to his bedroom. He gently placed Kyle on the bed, who shuffled backwards to get comfortable. Samuel followed him, lying down next to Kyle and facing him while Kyle turned onto his side. Samuel reached out and gently traced the inked lines on Kyle's chest as he leant in, capturing his lips in a kiss and teasing him with his tongue. Kyle slipped one of his legs in- between Samuel's and rubbed his thigh against Samuel's hard cock. When Samuel moaned into their kiss, Kyle gently rolled them over so he was lying on top of Samuel. He broke the kiss and kissed his way down to Samuel's nipples, sucking one into his mouth and playing with the barbell while teasing the other nipple with his fingers.

Kyle teased Samuel's nipples a bit longer, loving to hear him moan and see him arch his back in pleasure. He kissed his way down, trailing the fine line of hair until he reached the top of his boxers.

Looking up at Samuel, he waited until Samuel opened his eyes and looked at Kyle. He hooked his fingers into Samuel's boxers and asked, "Can I?"

"Yes," Samuel moaned breathlessly.

Kyle pulled Samuel's boxers down and hummed in pleasant surprise as he discovered another piercing. He quickly kissed the tip of his cock and then flicked his tongue against the barbell; Samuel groaning in pleasure. Then Kyle slowly licked his way down the whole shaft until he reached Samuel's balls and sucked them into his mouth, playing with them. He took Samuel's cock into his mouth and sucked on it, occasionally flicking his tongue against the slit and the barbell. When Kyle had settled on a rhythm, he slipped his hand into his own boxers and started stroking his own cock in sync with sucking on Samuel's cock, moaning around it.

Samuel opened his eyes when he felt Kyle moaning around his cock. When he noticed Kyle was stroking himself, he tried to bat his hand away. When that didn't work, he called out his name.

"Did I hurt you?" Kyle had stopped immediately when he heard Samuel calling his name. He looked at him worriedly.

"No. I just wanted you to stop jerking yourself off. I want to do that," Samuel smiled at Kyle as he gently caressed his cheek and then ran his hand through Kyle's hair.

Kyle returned the smile while pulling his hand out of his boxers. He went back to sucking Samuel's cock, paying special attention to the head and the barbell. It didn't take that much longer until Samuel mumbled that he was going to come. He did just seconds later; Kyle swallowing everything. Kyle let Samuel's cock slip out of his mouth and then crawled up, lying down next to him and propping himself up on his elbow. He watched Samuel, whose cheeks were flushed and chest was heaving, trying to regain his normal breathing.

"You're beautiful," Kyle said softly and then he was swept into another kiss by Samuel who rolled Kyle onto his back. He then trailed his hand down over Kyle's chest and abs before his hand disappeared into Kyle's boxers, wrapping it around his cock. He stroked his cock in a fast, steady rhythm, and every time he swept his thumb over the slit, Kyle moaned loudly while arching his back. It only took a couple of strokes until Kyle cried out in orgasm as Samuel could feel his come spilling all over his hand. He then pulled it out of Kyle's boxers before licking his hand clean and then leaning in to kiss Kyle, sharing both their tastes.

Kyle lay panting on the bed while Samuel got up and disappeared in his en-suite, returning with a wet cloth. He gently patted Kyle's hip, encouraging him to lift his hips. He took off his boxers before wiping him clean. When Samuel returned from the bathroom after dropping off the cloth, he lay down next to Kyle, facing him, while gently caressing his cheek.

"Are you okay?"

"Perfect," Kyle opened his eyes as he turned his head to look at Samuel and then grinned at him.

"Do you want to go to sleep yet?" Samuel asked, remembering that Kyle had to be up earlier than him.

"No. We could switch the TV on for a while. Although, I'm not sure how long I can keep my eyes open, but I want to spend some more time with you before I fall asleep."

"Okay. Have you set your alarm for the morning?" When Kyle had nodded, Samuel got up again and pulled the duvet aside on his side before encouraging Kyle to lift himself up so Samuel could do the same on his side. Samuel grabbed the remotes, switching the TV on, and then slipped back into bed, pulling the duvet up to their waists. Kyle snuggled into his side and made himself comfortable with his head on Samuel's chest. It wasn't long until Kyle slipped his arm around Samuel's waist and his leg between Samuel's. He drifted off to sleep shortly after.

Samuel switched off the TV when he was sure that Kyle was fast asleep. He then placed a soft kiss into his hair before he closed his eyes, falling asleep shortly after.

Kyle groaned when his alarm went off, usually leaving it on until he got up. When he remembered that he was at Samuel's place, he untangled himself immediately and turned the alarm off straight away, not wanting to disturb Samuel too much.

Kyle snuck out of the bedroom and made his way into the main bathroom to get ready before heading down to the kitchen to make some coffee for work. He was surprised when he saw Samuel in the kitchen preparing coffee and toast for him.

"Morning. What are you doing up?" Kyle asked as he appreciated the sight of Samuel just wearing boxers.

"Good morning," Samuel smiled at Kyle as he handed him a cup of coffee and a plate with toast on it. "I'm making sure you're eating breakfast. Do you take food to work?"

"I can just buy something."

"Go eat, I'll make lunch for you," Samuel said as he stepped closer to Kyle and placed a chaste kiss on his lips before nudging him in the direction of the chairs.

"You don't have to, Samuel."

"Shh, it's no problem. Is the rest of the lasagna okay for your lunch?"

"Yes, that's perfect."

"And coffee for the thermos?"

"Please. Thank you," Kyle mumbled, as he had just taken a bite of the toast.

When Samuel had placed the container with the food and the thermos on the table, Kyle held out his hand to him and pulled Samuel onto his lap as soon as he had taken his hand. Samuel wrapped one of his arms around Kyle's neck while Kyle wrapped one arm around Samuel's waist and cupped his face with the other hand, pulling Samuel in for a kiss. Kyle slowly let his hand wander into Samuel's hair, his fingertips teasing at the nape of his neck while their tongues fought playfully with each other.

Kyle broke the kiss after a short while, both of them being slightly out of breath as they rested their foreheads against one another.

"I need to go to work."

"Are you coming around after work tomorrow?" Samuel knew he wouldn't be able to see Kyle this evening as Kyle was having dinner with his family.

"I'd love to if it's okay."

"Of course, it is. Just bring some clothes to stay over again, okay?"

Kyle nodded and then kissed Samuel one last time before Samuel got up and Kyle finally left for work.

It was Friday evening when Kyle and Samuel were lying on Samuel's couch, Samuel spooning Kyle as they were watching TV. Kyle got a text message from Julius asking him if he was still going to pick him and Ben up from the airport the next morning.

Kyle groaned quietly, holding the phone up to Samuel so he could read the message and then turned slightly to look at him. "I'd completely forgotten about that. Do you want to come along when I pick them up?"

"Do you want to tell them about us? Or am I assuming things here?"

"Of course, you're not. I want to be with you. And I don't mind telling them, but we don't have to if you're not comfortable with it. But to be fair, it probably won't take Julius long to figure it out. He knows me too well."

"I'd prefer it if we didn't tell them straight away. Ben can be a bit overprotective as well."

"That's absolutely fine. And it's not just Ben, Julius is protective of you as well."

"What?" Samuel looked perplexed and Kyle turned around properly, gently stroking Samuel's cheek.

"Yeah, he talked to me as well."

"What did he tell you?"

"He just told me that you're not a one-night stand kind of guy and that I should leave you alone if that was all I was after." When Samuel still looked shocked, Kyle continued, "You didn't expect Julius to be protective of you?"

"No, not really. I mean I know we get along, but I always thought that was because I'm friends with Ben."

"I think he values your friendship. I'm guessing you were always there for them when they needed it. Just don't be mad at Julius."

"I'm not mad at him," Samuel leant in to kiss Kyle, teasing his lips open with his tongue before seeking out Kyle's to play with it. Kyle's hand wandered into Samuel's hair, holding him in place while they kissed. Samuel tightened his hold on Kyle's waist so he wouldn't roll off the couch.

Kyle broke the kiss shortly after when he remembered that Julius was probably waiting for a reply from him. "I should text Julius back and let him know that I'll pick them up. I won't mention you coming along yet."

"Don't you think you should tell him I'm coming along?"

"No, he'll be more suspicious then. If I don't tell him and just bring you along tomorrow I can tell him that we had made plans."

"Okay. You know him better."

Chapter Six

Julius and Benjamin had just retrieved their luggage and made their way outside, looking for Kyle in the arrivals hall, who they found leaning against a pillar chatting to a guy.

Julius rolled his eyes, not being impressed that Kyle used the time waiting for them to flirt with some guy until he stopped dead in his tracks when he realized the guy was Samuel. He pulled Benjamin to a stop and then pointed out Kyle and Samuel, who appeared to be in a deep conversation, and he gave Ben a confused look.

"I take it you didn't know Kyle was bringing Samuel?" Ben asked while still watching them. He was surprised to see both of them here and how relaxed Samuel seemed to be around Kyle.

"No, Kyle didn't mention that. Although I shouldn't be that surprised because he was really interested in Samuel at our wedding."

"True. Come on then, let's go over to them," Ben grabbed Julius hand again and they made their way over to Kyle and Samuel. Kyle just noticed them when they'd nearly reached them.

Julius watched as a huge grin appeared on Kyle's face and he bounced over to them, wrapping Julius into a tight hug. "It's good to see you back. Did you have a nice honeymoon?"

"It was amazing. I just wish it had been longer," Julius said as he pulled back from the hug and then watched Kyle hugging Ben as well while Samuel gave Julius a quick hug and a welcome back as well.

"Let's get you home. You can tell me all about your honeymoon next time I see you," Kyle grabbed one of the suitcases and started pulling it in the direction of the car park. Julius had to jog up to him to catch him so he could walk with Kyle while Ben and Samuel followed further behind.

"Do you want to tell me something?" Julius asked curiously, as he looked at Kyle, but he wasn't able to tell if Kyle and Samuel were just friends or if there was more.

"Should I?" Kyle asked innocently, while giving Julius an angelic smile.

"Care to explain why you brought Samuel along?"

"We had plans for today. And to be honest I'd forgotten that I was supposed to pick you up so I just asked Samuel if he wanted to come along."

"So you're friends now?"

"Yeah. We've met up a couple of times since your wedding and I really like him," Kyle knew that denying his feelings for Samuel would make Julius suspicious. He was telling the truth after all; he was just leaving out a few bits.

"Good. He likes you too, he's very relaxed around you," Julius threw his arm around Kyle and pulled him in, placing a kiss on his cheek.

When they'd dropped off Julius and Benjamin at their house, Julius invited Kyle and Samuel to come around for dinner in the evening so they could tell them all about their honeymoon.

Kyle was torn. On the one side, he wanted to spend more time with Samuel alone, but he was curious to hear about the honeymoon as well. In the end, he just asked Samuel if it was okay if they changed their original plan, not giving away that it was supposed to be a date, and Samuel agreed straight away.

Kyle and Samuel left after agreeing on a time and then went back to Samuel's place, just happy to be spending time with each other.

They left Samuel's place shortly after 6 p.m. It was only a ten-minute walk to Julius and Ben's house. They hadn't been walking for long when Samuel noticed that Kyle had attempted to take his hand several times, but always pulled back at the last second. Samuel wasn't sure if Kyle didn't dare to take his hand or if he was just being considerate, but Samuel didn't care. He grabbed Kyle's hand, intertwining their fingers. He felt Kyle squeezing his hand and when a smile appeared on Kyle's face, Samuel leant in and placed a kiss on his cheek, whispering, "You can tell them about us if you want."

"Are you sure?" Kyle looked surprised, but he was satisfied when Samuel nodded confidently. "Okay. I won't tell them unless they say something," Kyle lifted their joined hands and placed a gentle kiss on the back of Samuel's hand just as they turned into Julius and Ben's street.

Kyle let go of Samuel's hand when they reached the house and then he rang the doorbell, Julius opening the door shortly after and letting them in before hugging both of them quickly. Julius led them into the kitchen where Ben was finishing dinner and told them to sit down at the table already.

"Do you want a beer, Samuel?"

"Please."

"Kyle, are you staying over so you can have a drink?"

"No, I won't stay here. But I'll have a beer as well." Julius looked confused as Kyle normally stayed the night when he drank. "I'm staying at Samuel's, I'm sure you two will be glad to be alone on your first night back home."

Benjamin raised an eyebrow questioningly as he looked at Samuel, not expecting them to be this close already. Julius handed both of them a beer.

"What? Is it that strange that I'm letting Kyle stay the night at mine?"

"Of course not, it's just unusual for you," Ben said.

Samuel rolled his eyes; he was getting sick of everyone being overprotective of him. "I think I can judge for myself if I trust Kyle or not. And it really shouldn't surprise you that I do seeing that your husband is best friends with Kyle."

"I didn't mean it in a bad way, Samuel. And of course you can trust Kyle; he's a great guy and friend."

Samuel was about to reply when Kyle reached over and took his hand, squeezing it tightly. "It's okay; it's not worth fighting about." It was only when Kyle realized Julius and Ben were staring at their joined hands that he noticed what he had done and he tried to pull his hand back, but Samuel turned his hand around and intertwined their fingers. "Shit, I'm sorry, Samuel."

"You don't have anything to be sorry about," Samuel leant in and placed a kiss on Kyle's cheek before he turned his attention to Ben and Julius. "We started dating last week."

"I knew it!" Julius exclaimed as he smiled at them. "I'm so happy for both of you."

"Thanks," Kyle smiled brightly at Julius, and Samuel knew it had been the right decision not to keep their relationship secret. But when Kyle looked at Ben, he didn't know what to expect. He didn't mind Ben being protective of Samuel and it surely couldn't be worse than Alex, but he still held his breath until Ben spoke.

"I'm happy for both of you as well," Ben gave them a genuine smile, showing them that he meant it. "Have you met Alex yet?" Ben wasn't sure how much Kyle knew and he didn't want to accidentally give something away.

"Yes," Kyle laughed at the memory of it. "And I've been warned not to hurt Samuel. So if you want to do the same, now is your chance."

"I don't think there's anything to add if Alex spoke to you already, you should fear Alex more than me."

"I don't think Kyle needs to fear Alex. Both Alex and Mike like Kyle and they get along nicely," Samuel intervened as he gently squeezed Kyle's hand.

After dinner, they spent the evening in the living room, Julius and Ben telling them about their honeymoon and showing them pictures of it. Kyle cuddled into Samuel's side as soon as they sat down on the couch. Samuel put his arm around Kyle's shoulder and pulled him in even closer, placing a soft kiss into his hair as Kyle squeezed his thigh in thanks.

It was just gone 10 p.m. when Kyle and Samuel decided to head back to Samuel's place. They said their goodbyes, Julius insisting that he and Kyle needed to have a proper catch-up at some point with only the two of them.

They slowly walked back to Samuel's house, their hands being intertwined the whole time and Kyle rubbing his thumb over the back of Samuel's hand. When they reached the house and Samuel had let them in, Kyle turned to Samuel and cupped his face in his hands, pulling him close and kissing him passionately.

Samuel broke their frantic kissing when he slid his hands under Kyle's shirt and then let them glide to his ass, squeezing tightly as he suggested, "I think we should take this to the bedroom."

There was no way Kyle could take this the wrong way, and as soon as he nodded, Samuel grabbed his hand and pulled him upstairs and into his bedroom. Kyle excused himself to go to the bathroom and Samuel took his chance to grab a different piercing for his tongue. Samuel went into the main bathroom, but instead of using the toilet he replaced his current tongue piercing with a vibrating one.

When Samuel came back to the bedroom, Kyle was lying on his bed naked, slowly, teasingly stroking his cock as he looked at Samuel while biting his lip. Samuel got rid of his clothes before joining Kyle on the bed and gently batting Kyle's hand away so he could take a hold of Kyle's cock, stroking it while sucking on the tip, being mindful not to use his tongue. Samuel used his other hand to tease at Kyle's hole, letting one finger circle it before slightly pushing in, Kyle moaning out loud.

Samuel let Kyle's cock fall from his lips and then spread his ass cheeks so he could tease the entrance with his tongue before pushing his tongue in completely, Kyle gasping in surprise when he felt the vibrations of Samuel's tongue piercing.

"Fuck, Sam, what the hell is that?"

Samuel grinned when he pulled back and then stuck his tongue out so Kyle could see his piercing. "Vibrating barbell. I thought you'd like that."

"Mmhm," Kyle hummed as he made grabby hands for Samuel, who shuffled up the bed and then leant down to kiss Kyle. Kyle dived into the kiss and immediately sought out his tongue, playing around with the piercing as Samuel moaned softly into their kiss. "Fuck me," Kyle breathed as they broke the kiss and he looked at Samuel, who stared back at him with big blue eyes while biting his lip. "It's okay, we don't have to have sex if you don't want to," Kyle said as he gently cupped Samuel's face and stroked his cheeks with his thumbs.

"It's not that, I do want to. It's just that I haven't topped in ages."

"Would you like to top? Or would you rather bottom? Or we could just get each other off."

"I'd love to top." Samuel licked his lips before he leant down to kiss Kyle and then pulled back again, looking for lube and a condom in his bedside drawer.

Kyle spread his legs wide and then groaned when he felt Samuel's tongue dipping into his hole again. The vibrations of the piercing went straight to his cock, which was leaking pre-come already. When Samuel had teased Kyle enough with his tongue, he grabbed the lube and coated three of his fingers generously before sliding one in, gently opening Kyle while lazily stroking his cock.

When Samuel had worked three fingers into Kyle, he was satisfied with how open he was and withdrew his fingers. Kyle groaned at the loss of them, and Samuel grabbed the condom. He was just about to open it when Kyle took it out of his hand and tore it open before rolling it down over Samuel's cock and giving it a few strokes. Samuel moaned quietly when Kyle flicked his thumb against his piercing.

Samuel positioned his cock at Kyle's entrance, the tip just nudging the tight ring of muscles, and then stopped to look at Kyle, who nodded eagerly as he wrapped his legs around Samuel's waist. Samuel slowly pushed the tip of his cock in and then waited so Kyle could adjust, but Kyle rocked his hips in Samuel's direction and pulled him closer with his legs causing Samuel to slide in further, moaning at how tight Kyle felt around him. Kyle didn't stop pulling him closer until Samuel was all the way in, stilling when he saw Samuel biting his lip before burying his face in Kyle's neck.

"Okay?" Kyle asked as he stroked over Samuel's back.

"Mmhm. I'm just not sure how long I'm going to last, you feel so good."

"So do you, but don't hold back on my account," Kyle whispered as he placed a kiss into Samuel's hair while gently scratching his nails down Samuel's back, who groaned quietly.

Samuel slowly started rocking his hips as he lifted his head out of Kyle's neck and gazed down at him, leaning down for a messy kiss. When Kyle broke the kiss, he groaned and begged for more. Samuel shifted slightly and thrust in faster, Kyle crying out in pleasure when he hit his prostate.

"Tell me if I'm too rough," Samuel said as he looked at Kyle, his thrusts becoming erratic, but Kyle only shook his head as beautiful moans fell from his lips. He tightened the hold his legs had around Samuel's waist.

Kyle could tell that Samuel was close so he started playing with both of his nipple piercings. Samuel's moans becoming louder as Samuel grabbed Kyle's cock and stroked it in the same frantic rhythm of his thrusts, not wanting to neglect Kyle. When Samuel felt Kyle clenching his muscles around his cock, he couldn't hold back any longer, coming with a quiet gasp and Kyle cried out in orgasm a few seconds later. Samuel collapsed on top of Kyle, both of them coming down from their high as Kyle soothingly stroked Samuel's hair and back. Their heartbeats slowing down to a normal rate again. When Samuel had his breath back, he lifted himself off Kyle, his cock slipping out as he rolled onto his side. Kyle gasped at the loss he felt when Samuel slid out.

"God, that was amazing," Kyle rolled onto his side as well so he was facing Samuel and then kissed him gently, all the need for urgency gone now.

"It really was. Are you sure I wasn't too rough?"

"Of course, you weren't. I loved it and the fact that you surprised me."

"Thought I would be reserved in bed, too?"

"Yes, even though I probably shouldn't have," Kyle chuckled softly as he stroked through Samuel's hair.

Samuel kissed Kyle's forehead before getting up and disposing of the used condom on his way to the bathroom, where he replaced the vibrating barbell with his normal one. He then went back into the bedroom, cleaning Kyle with a damp cloth. Both of them slipped under the covers afterwards and cuddled into each other. Kyle nearly wrapped himself around Samuel as they slowly drifted off to sleep.

Kyle woke to an empty bed and he groaned when he saw it was after 11 a.m. already. He slipped out of bed and into a pair of boxers before making his way downstairs to find Samuel. The music that was softly playing in the kitchen gave away Samuel's location and Kyle made his way there. A lovely smell of cooking hanging in the air as he padded into the kitchen barefoot. His feet made no sound as he walked up behind Samuel and then wrapped his arms around his waist. He couldn't help noticing that Samuel tensed up.

Samuel had woken up early, and when Kyle showed no sign of waking up any time soon, he decided to head downstairs and cook some dinners so he could freeze them. He was just stirring the simmering soup as he felt a pair of arms wrapping around him and he automatically tensed up. He relaxed again as soon as he realized it was Kyle, leaning back into the embrace slightly.

"Morning. Why didn't you wake me?" Kyle kissed Samuel's cheek before Samuel turned around in his arms and then cupped his face in his hand, kissing Kyle softly.

"You obviously needed the sleep. I didn't think I'd get out of bed without waking you, but you barely stirred."

"Sorry."

"It's fine. Would you like some breakfast?"

"Coffee?" Kyle looked at Samuel with a hopeful expression.

"Of course," Samuel kissed the tip of Kyle's nose. "Would you like some scrambled eggs on toast as well? Or do you want something else?"

"Scrambled eggs on toast are fine. Thanks, Sam. Sorry, is it okay if I call you Sam?"

"Sure, I don't mind. Go and sit down, I'll make you breakfast."

✦

Chapter Seven

It was a month later when Kyle and Samuel were at Julius and Ben's place. They'd been invited to a gathering of quite a few friends, although Julius and Ben had offered that they could come by on a different day. Samuel didn't want Kyle to neglect his friends either so he agreed to come.

Samuel was sat on the couch chatting to Ben when Kyle wandered up to them and sat down on the arm of the couch, squeezing Samuel's arm lightly.

"Are you okay?"

"Yes, I'm fine. Go back to your friends, Kyle," Samuel smiled at Kyle as he squeezed the hand that was lying on his arm.

Kyle did as he was told and wandered back over to where Julius was chatting to Danny, Carlos and Roberto. He joined the conversation again, Julius leaving shortly after to chat to some other friends, and Danny came over to Kyle.

"So are you finally done being all friendly with Ben's friend?"

"His name is Samuel and he's my friend as well."

"You just think he's hot. And I can see why you do, he's very handsome. I hope you got him out of your system after fucking him."

"Fuck off, Danny! I'm not going to listen to you bad mouthing Samuel. And even if that was the case, I still wouldn't be interested in you," Kyle's raised voice drew Julius' attention and he came rushing over to see what the problem was.

"Kyle, what's the matter?" Julius asked as he looked at Kyle.

"I'm sorry for raising my voice, but I don't think I can be friends with someone who insults my boyfriend."

"You're dating him?" Danny asked, shock written all over his face and his tone judgmental.

Kyle growled at Danny and Julius grabbed him before he could do something stupid. "When will you finally understand that I'm not interested in you?"

"Calm down, Kyle. You don't want to scare Samuel, do you?" Julius asked quietly. He could see Kyle's demeanor soften immediately at the mention of Samuel, Kyle shaking his head ever so slightly. Julius turned to see where Ben and Samuel were, and when he couldn't see them anywhere, he asked Roberto to get them.

When Ben and Samuel came into the living room, they immediately rushed over to where Julius was still holding onto Kyle.

"What happened?" Samuel asked.

Julius could clearly see the concern on Samuel's face as he approached them. Kyle struggled to get out of Julius' hold and sought out Samuel's touch straight away.

"Kyle will tell you. Will you take him upstairs, please?"

Samuel nodded as he wrapped his arm around Kyle, pulling him close. He guided him upstairs to one of the guest rooms, turning his head to place a soft kiss on Kyle's temple before asking, "What happened, Kyle?"

"I don't even know where to start. Can we lie down? I'll tell you then," Kyle pulled off his shirt when Samuel had nodded and then tugged at the hem of Samuel's shirt. "Do you mind taking your shirt off as well?"

"Of course, I don't mind," Kyle pulled off Samuel's shirt immediately. He dragged him over to the bed, Samuel lying down on it before Kyle crawled up next to him and he snuggled into his side. Kyle rested his head on Samuel's chest and gently played with his nipple piercings while Samuel ran his hand through Kyle's hair and over his back soothingly.

"Danny likes me, you probably noticed that at the wedding, but I'm not interested in him. He's known that from the beginning and I thought we could be friends even though he always tries to flirt with me. I've never returned his advances and I didn't see the harm in him being flirty with me, but it has gotten so much worse since I started showing an interest in you. He thought I'd only be interested in you for a one-night stand and that I'd have gotten you out of my system by now. That's what he said to me earlier, and when I told him I couldn't be friends with someone who insults my boyfriend, he lost it. I lost it at that point as well, but Julius interfered and stopped me doing something stupid. Are you mad at me?"

Kyle lifted his head so he was able to look at Samuel, but he only saw understanding and affection in Samuel's eyes, who smiled at him warmly.

"Why would I be?" Samuel quickly kissed Kyle on the lips before Kyle rested his head on his chest again.

They were interrupted by a knock on the door. Julius and Ben entered the guest room when Samuel had called out that they could come in.

"Are you okay, Kyle?"

"He's fine," Samuel eventually answered when Kyle showed no sign of responding and he gently patted his ass, continuing, "aren't you?"

"Yes, I'm fine. But just so you know I'm not coming to your place again when Danny is here."

"Fair enough. Everyone is gone now anyway so you don't have to worry about that at the moment."

"You're wearing your nipple piercings again?" Ben asked, shock written all over his face as he realized Kyle was playing with Samuel's piercings.

"Yes. Well, they're not the same ones; these are new."

"Shit, I'm sorry, Samuel," Ben could have slapped himself when he realized what he had said and he didn't know how much Kyle knew.

"It's okay, don't worry about it."

"Do you want to stay here tonight?" Samuel knew that Julius' question was only partly directed at him. Although he never stayed at Julius and Ben's, he was willing to make an exception for Kyle's sake. But he could already feel Kyle shaking his head.

"No. And I think we should head back to your place now," Kyle said as he lifted his head, directing the last part towards Samuel, who nodded in agreement.

When they had both put their shirts back on, they said their goodbyes to Julius and Ben, heading back to Samuel's place.

"I'm so sorry I asked you to come along when everyone else was at Julius and Ben's anyway," Kyle gently rubbed circles into the back of Samuel's hand with his thumb.

"You don't need to apologize. I could have said no," Samuel squeezed Kyle's hand as he leant over and kissed his cheek.

"Yeah, but you only agreed to it because of me."

"That may be true, but it wasn't that bad anyway. I actually enjoyed it," Kyle looked at Samuel with a doubtful expression on his face and Samuel smiled softly before continuing, "I enjoyed it because I got to see you being all happy, and if you're happy, I'm happy, too."

Samuel let go of Kyle's hand and then wrapped his arm around Kyle's shoulder, pulling him into his side and kissing his temple as they walked the rest of the way home.

Kyle was woken up by Samuel thrashing around the bed and pleading for someone not to do something to him. When Kyle tried to calm Samuel down by stroking through his hair and then tried to grab his hands, Samuel woke up with a start.

"Don't touch me!" Samuel shouted as he roughly slapped Kyle's hands away, tears streaming down his face, and Kyle let go immediately and then backed off.

"Shh, it's okay. I won't touch you if you don't want me to," Kyle spoke softly, quietly, so not to scare Samuel even more. He watched him cowering on the edge of the bed. "Is there anything I can do to help you?" Kyle felt useless. He had no idea how to help Samuel and he hated to see him like this.

"Call Alex," was all Samuel said between gasps for air and Kyle nodded in understanding.

"Okay, I will call Alex. I'm going to have to use your phone." Kyle thought it was best if he let Samuel know what he was doing and then grabbed Samuel's mobile, looking for Alex's number, dialing it straight away when he found it. It rang a couple of times until a very tired sounding Alex answered.

"Samuel? Is everything okay?"

"It's Kyle. I'm sorry for waking you, but I think Samuel had a nightmare. He won't let me near him and I don't know what to do."

"Shit, I'm coming over right now! Just stay with him. Distract him, ask him questions. That's all you can do for now."

"Okay. Thanks, Alex." Kyle placed Samuel's phone back on the nightstand when Alex had hung up and then sat down on the edge of the bed furthest away from Samuel. "Alex is on his way," Kyle told Samuel before he did as he was told by Alex. He started asking Samuel any question that came to his mind.

It only took about five minutes until Kyle could hear Alex entering the house with the key he had. He waited for him to enter the bedroom, being surprised when he saw Mike as well.

"Go with Mike, Kyle. I'll take care of Samuel," Kyle couldn't help but notice that Alex sounded rather cold towards him before giving his full attention to Samuel. Kyle did as he was told and went downstairs with Mike.

"Hey, don't mind Alex; he's just worried about Samuel," Mike told him as he returned with a glass of water for Kyle. "What happened?"

"I think Samuel had a nightmare and when he woke up, he slapped my hands away, telling me not to touch him. I backed off and then called Alex."

It only took fifteen minutes until Samuel and Alex appeared in the living room. Samuel's tears having dried, but his eyes looked all red and puffy. Kyle stood up immediately, but then hesitated; not sure if he should approach Samuel or not.

"Are you okay?" Kyle sounded so worried. Samuel gave him a tiny smile, holding out his arms for Kyle, who rushed into the embrace immediately.

"I'm fine, just a bit embarrassed," Samuel whispered as Kyle wrapped his arms around him tightly.

"There's no need for you to be embarrassed," Kyle whispered before placing a soft kiss on Samuel's jaw.

Alex watched on in confusion as Samuel held out his arms for Kyle and then clung onto him tightly as they were whispering to each other. Alex was startled out of his thoughts when he felt Mike's arms wrapping around his waist from behind. Mike placed his chin on Alex's shoulder as he whispered, "I think you jumped to conclusions again, ace. I don't think this was Kyle's fault."

Alex nodded in agreement. "I think I owe him an apology."

"He won't mind, he can see that you're concerned about Samuel and that you only want what's best for him," Mike gently kissed Alex's neck as Alex relaxed into Mike's arms.

Alex watched as Kyle pulled out of their embrace and took a small step back. Samuel reached out for his hand and intertwined their fingers, not being willing to let Kyle go.

"I'm not going anywhere," Kyle spoke softly, but Alex and Mike were still able to hear him as they watched Kyle guiding Samuel to the couch. Kyle sat down and pulled Samuel down next to him. Samuel let himself be pulled into Kyle's side, burying his face in Kyle's neck. Kyle soothingly stroked through Samuel's hair and over his back while placing soft little kisses into Samuel's hair.

Alex pulled out of Mike's embrace and made his way over to Samuel and Kyle. He knew he needed to apologize to Kyle before they could even think about going home. He sat down on the coffee table, facing them, but neither of them seemed to notice him.

"Kyle?" Alex asked, continuing when Kyle looked at him, "I'm sorry for the way I spoke to you earlier."

"It's fine, I know you were worried about Samuel."

"I still shouldn't have jumped to the conclusion that this was your fault. I'm sorry for that, too."

"You blamed Kyle for this?" Samuel lifted his head so he was able to look at Alex, who looked back at him sheepishly.

"What was I supposed to think? Kyle called me in a panic and told me you wouldn't let him near you." Alex shrugged helplessly, but Samuel could see that he regretted blaming Kyle. He softened slightly as Alex turned back to Kyle. "You did the right thing by calling me."

"I only did what Samuel told me to do."

Alex's head whipped back to Samuel and he looked at him stunned. "You responded to Kyle?"

"Uh…" Samuel took a few seconds to try to remember what had happened. "I did. When I told you not to touch me you let go immediately. Then you asked if there was anything you could do to help me and I told you to call Alex. I also answered your questions. Shit, I slapped your hands. Did I hurt you?" Samuel looked at Kyle with a worried expression on his face, but Kyle just shook his head.

"No, you didn't. Is it unusual that you responded to me?"

"Kind of, I only ever used to respond to Alex. Although I haven't had a panic attack in over a year now," Samuel explained. He knew that Kyle must have a million questions for him, but he wanted to talk to him alone when Alex and Mike had left.

"What triggered this, Samuel?" Alex needed to know what caused the panic attack. He didn't need Samuel to start having them again. Although with Samuel responding to Kyle, Alex was sure Kyle could calm him down if it ever happened again.

"I think it was a comment Ben made that caused the nightmare about that night."

"Ben should know better."

"He didn't do it on purpose and he apologized immediately," Samuel untangled himself from Kyle and then leant over to Alex, pulling him into a hug. "Thanks for coming over and calming me down."

"Anything for you. Although you probably wouldn't have needed me."

"I still appreciate your support."

"Glad to hear that. Talk to Kyle, yeah?" Alex whispered the last part into Samuel's ear, and when Samuel had agreed, he pulled back. He looked at Samuel for a few seconds before leaning in and pecking his lips lightly. Alex knew Mike wouldn't comment on it as he had seen them doing this before and he knew it was just a platonic kiss. Alex wasn't sure how Kyle would react. When he glanced at Kyle, Alex was relieved that Kyle didn't seem to mind; his expression not having changed in the slightest.

"Thank you too, Mike. And I'm sorry for dragging both of you out of bed in the middle of the night."

"Shush, you idiot. You don't need to apologize," Alex ruffled Samuel's hair as he got up. "But we are going home now."

Samuel licked his lips nervously as he looked at Kyle when Alex and Mike had left. He grabbed Kyle's hand and intertwined their fingers. "Let's go back to bed."

"Do you think you can go back to sleep?" It was just approaching 4:30 a.m., but Kyle doubted that Samuel would be able to go back to sleep.

"Probably not, but I want to be comfortable when I tell you what happened."

"You don't have to tell me if you don't want to." Even though Kyle's mind was racing with all the questions he'd like an answer to, he wasn't going to make Samuel even more uncomfortable.

"I want to tell you, it's only fair. And I don't have a problem talking about it. The reason I had a panic attack was because I relived what happened in the nightmare." When Kyle nodded in understanding, Samuel tugged on his hand and pulled him upstairs to his bedroom, both of them slipping back into bed.

"How do you want to do this?" Kyle asked as he sat cross- legged on the bed and he looked at Samuel, who was leaning against the headboard.

"Are you comfortable to sit like this? This could take a while." When Kyle had agreed that he was indeed fine to sit like that, Samuel reached out and took one of Kyle's hands into his, gently playing with his fingers as he started talking quietly.

Samuel told him that he had been in a relationship with a guy called Jason about two and a half years ago. The relationship had been good or so Samuel had thought at the time, even though it should have been a warning for Samuel that Alex had never warmed up to Jason. It was half a year into the relationship when things had started to change. Jason began to be a lot more forceful during sex, and while Samuel didn't mind a bit of roughness, it was painful more often than not. Although, he did put it down to the heat of the moment as Jason had never hurt him on purpose.

That was until Jason was drunk one night when Samuel came to his place, both of them ending up in bed together and Jason pinning Samuel down while restraining both of his arms with one of his. Samuel had tried to fight against the hold, but it was useless as Jason was heavier than Samuel and he had a lot more muscles. When Samuel called out for help, Jason hit his jaw in an attempt to shut him up. When that didn't work, he roughly tugged on one of Samuel's nipple piercings, knowing how sensitive he was to them and hoping that would silence him. But he tugged so hard on it that he ripped it out. Samuel cried out in pain, finally being able to free himself due to the adrenalin rush, as he kicked Jason in the groin. Once Samuel was free, he quickly picked up his shirt, glad that he was still wearing his jeans, and fled Jason's apartment.

Samuel took out his mobile and called Alex, not knowing what else to do as the pain of his bruised jaw and the ripped nipple set in. When Alex answered the call, Samuel only had to tell him that he'd had a fight with Jason and Alex agreed to pick him up straight away.

They arrived at Alex and Mike's place about 20 minutes later. Alex gasped in shock when he saw that Samuel's jaw was red and starting to swell, not needing to ask if Jason had hit him. He was even more shocked when he saw the blood on Samuel's shirt after he'd taken off his jacket and then discovered that Jason had ripped out one of Samuel's piercings. Not wasting any time, Alex convinced Samuel to let him drive to the hospital to get it checked out and bandaged up so it could heal properly.

Kyle was lost for words, but Samuel didn't even give him a chance to say anything anyway as he continued talking.

"I stayed with Alex and Mike for a while, but I started having nightmares about that night, which triggered the panic attacks. I didn't let anyone near me then, except for Alex. If anyone else did touch me, I would tense up immediately."

"Is that why you tense up when I touch you when you're not aware of my presence?"

"You're very observant. Yes, it is. But please don't think I'm afraid of your touch, it's just an unconscious reaction."

"I know, you do relax when you realize it's me. How long did you stay with Alex and Mike?"

"About three months. The nightmares and panic attacks didn't stop, but I didn't want to be a burden to them. Not that it was any use because Alex practically moved in with me here. I couldn't stand the thought of living in my apartment, where Jason knew the address to, so I ended up buying this house. When the nightmares and panic attacks still didn't stop, I went to therapy. That helped me to get over it and I've been free of nightmares for nearly a year and a half now."

"I don't even know what to say. I can't believe what this guy did to you. Not that you can see that you had one of your piercings ripped out, I couldn't even tell you which one it was. They look the same to me."

"You can if you look closely. And you probably can't tell the difference because I took the other one out at that time as well and let them both heal. I only got them re-pierced about a year ago when I got my other two piercings done." When Kyle didn't answer, Samuel looked at the thoughtful expression on his face and then gently squeezed his fingers. "Please tell me this doesn't change anything."

"It does," Kyle said and Samuel's hold around his fingers slackened as he dropped his head. Samuel had feared that this would happen and he prepared himself for the rejection he was sure that was coming. He was surprised when he felt Kyle's other hand gently cupping his jaw and lifting his head up so Kyle could look at him as he said, "I admire you so much more now. You're so brave; I don't know how you're putting your trust in me. Have you been in a relationship since then?"

"No, I only had a couple of one-night stands. And I had to start trusting people again; I can't live my life being afraid that something might happen. You're making it very easy to trust you though. As I said you're very observant and you've always backed off if I was uncomfortable with something."

"But aren't you afraid that I might tug too hard on your barbells?"

"No. I enjoy when you tug on them, I wouldn't have gotten my nipples re-pierced if I didn't. I don't mind if it's a bit rougher either, you've never been so rough that it hurt. Okay?"

"Okay." Kyle still looked doubtful and Samuel feared he would be afraid to touch him now.

"Kyle, promise me you won't let what happened change the way you've treated me so far."

"I promise. But you have to promise as well that you'll let me know if I'm overstepping your boundaries and I don't notice."

"I promise, although I have no doubt that you would notice," Samuel gave Kyle a reassuring smile as he squeezed Kyle's hand gently and then leant in, kissing Kyle softly.

When they broke the kiss, Kyle stared at Samuel intently, but just as Samuel was about to question him, Kyle spoke softly, yet sincerely, "I love you, Samuel."

Samuel knew he loved Kyle as well when he felt a rush of warmth running through his body and his heart skipping a beat at hearing those precious words from Kyle. "I love you too, Kyle."

Samuel smiled softly when he saw Kyle's stunned expression, Kyle clearly not having expected Samuel to say it back. He let go of Kyle's hand so he could cup Kyle's face with both hands and he kissed him again; Kyle responding eagerly.

"Let's go back to sleep," Samuel suggested when Kyle yawned after they'd broken the kiss. He gently stroked over his cheek.

"Do you think you can go back to sleep?"

"I don't know, but I can give it a try."

"Okay. Will you wake me up if you can't sleep?"

"Yes, I will. I'd be glad for the company, but I'm hoping I'll be able to sleep."

When they'd both slipped under the covers again, Kyle inquired how Samuel wanted to sleep and Samuel told him it would be best if he was spooning Kyle. He wasn't sure if it was a good idea to sleep on his back with Kyle wrapping himself around him. Samuel had considered sleeping on their sides facing each other so they could hold each other, but he was sure that Kyle would find a way to wrap himself around Samuel. So, spooning Kyle seemed to be the safest option. Kyle didn't seem to mind their new sleeping position as Samuel pressed his chest against Kyle's back tightly and wrapped his arm around his waist. Kyle intertwined their fingers.

Kyle woke up to soft lips placing feather light kisses against his neck. He hummed in appreciation as he stretched his muscles.

"Good morning," Samuel whispered as he placed a gentle kiss just behind Kyle's ear.

When Kyle inquired if Samuel had been able to sleep, Samuel reassured him that he had indeed slept until about ten minutes ago. He told him that it was just gone 11 a.m. so Kyle knew they'd gotten a good few hours of sleep.

It was a Saturday a couple of weeks later as Kyle and Samuel left the florist. They'd been invited for lunch by Kyle's mum and Samuel had insisted that they should bring her some flowers. Samuel had also inquired if they could stop somewhere else before they made their way to Britt's house. When Kyle saw that Samuel had bought two more bouquets of flowers, he had a sinking feeling that he knew where Samuel was taking him.

When Samuel had pulled into the parking lot, he switched off the engine before turning to look at Kyle.

"Do you mind?"

"Of course not."

Both of them got out of the car and Samuel grabbed two of the flower bouquets, handing one to Kyle so he could still take his hand, lacing their fingers together. Samuel led the way until he came to a stop when they reached his parents' graves. When Kyle wanted to let go of his hand to give him some space, Samuel tightened his hold on him.

"Don't you want me to give you some space?" Kyle asked quietly as he gently rubbed his thumb over the back of Samuel's hand.

"No. Just stay where you are," Samuel let go of Kyle's hand so he could put the two flower bouquets down on the graves. He returned to Kyle's side and took a hold of his hand again, quietly telling Kyle about his parents' accident.

"I'm sorry about your parents," Kyle whispered when Samuel had finished talking. Samuel leaned in to kiss Kyle's temple gently.

Chapter Nine

It was Kyle's birthday and they were having a small party at Samuel's house after Samuel insisted that his place would be better as it was bigger. Samuel watched as Kyle was talking to a guy called Adrian with a big smile on his face; one that hadn't left his face since Adrian's surprise appearance. Seeing Kyle so happy made Samuel glad that he had decided to invite Adrian to Kyle's birthday without Kyle's knowledge.

When Kyle saw him, he waved him over and Samuel made his way over to them. He smiled as Kyle reached out for his hand as soon as he was close enough.

"Sam, this is Adrian. Adrian, this is my boyfriend, Samuel."

"It's nice to finally be able to put a face to your voice," Samuel laughed softly. He'd had the advantage that Kyle had shown him some pictures so he knew what Adrian looked like.

"What?" Kyle looked at them with a confused expression on his face.

"Your boyfriend invited me and he actually flew me in," Adrian explained to Kyle before he looked at Samuel, adding, "Which we have to talk about. There was no need to buy business class tickets for me!"

Samuel just shrugged his shoulders at Adrian, but he turned his attention to Kyle when he felt him tugging on his hand. He smiled at the stunned expression on Kyle's face.

"You flew Adrian in for me?" Kyle was amazed that Samuel would do something like that for him after they'd only been together for a couple of months. He was so happy to finally see Adrian again after such a long time. He knew that Adrian didn't really have the money to pay for the flight and Kyle had only been able to visit him a couple of times since Adrian and his family moved ten years ago.

"Yes," Samuel didn't get any further as he ended up with Kyle in his arms, who kissed him passionately. When Samuel broke the kiss, Kyle placed tiny kisses all over his face until Samuel eventually stopped him by gently taking hold of his face.

"Thank you so much, but this is too much. It's too expensive; you can't spend that much money on me."

"Are you happy to see Adrian again?" When Kyle nodded with a big smile on his face, Samuel continued, "Then it's not too much. And I think you'll find I can. It's not like I don't have the money, Kyle. Just see it as your birthday present from me."

"You better not have gotten me anything else!" Kyle said jokingly, before turning serious again, "Thank you. I love you."

"I love you too."

Kyle was still talking to Adrian while Samuel had excused himself to give them a bit of time together, when Jenson approached them.

"It's so good to see how happy Samuel makes you. I can see you're totally in love with each other by the way you're looking at each other."

"Yeah, he makes me very happy. He's an amazing man."

"How can you say that after such a short time?" Jenson interrupted their conversation.

"Because I love him and I have spent nearly all my time with him since I met him?"

"He hasn't even been at your apartment yet."

"But he has; not that it makes a difference. Just because you live in the same building doesn't mean you know everything, Jenson."

"Do you know your boyfriend is being kissed by some other guy right now?"

"I think you'll find I only kissed him on the cheek." Alex had heard enough. He didn't like the fact that this guy was trying to cause trouble between Samuel and Kyle, although he knew he didn't have anything to worry about when he heard Kyle's answers. "Although I'm pretty sure Kyle wouldn't bat an eyelid even if I had kissed Samuel on the lips. Hey, birthday boy." Alex grinned at Kyle as he turned his attention to him and Kyle laughed out loud.

"Hi, Alex. Where's Mike?"

"He's still at work, but he'll come over as soon as he's finished," Alex explained as he stepped closer to Kyle and then wrapped him into a tight hug before saying, "Happy Birthday, Kyle!" Alex placed a quick kiss on

Kyle's lips when he pulled back; nothing more than a peck. He really only wanted to prove a point to the judgmental prick.

"What the hell have you gotten involved in, Kyle?"

"The most amazing relationship I've ever had. But you know what? If you can't be happy for me you can get the hell out of Samuel's house, Jenson!"

Jenson looked taken aback by Kyle's outburst, but Kyle had had enough of his so called friends judging his relationship without even knowing Samuel properly. He decided he didn't need friends like that. Just as Jenson was going to reply, Samuel came over and handed Alex a drink before inquiring what was going on. Samuel didn't fail to notice that Kyle looked a lot less happy than he was when he left him alone with Adrian. He wondered what had happened.

Kyle's only reply was that he wanted Jenson to leave, which he did begrudgingly, before he told Samuel what had happened.

Kyle sat on the couch, cuddled into Samuel with Samuel's arm tightly wrapped around his shoulder, as they were chatting to Alex, Mike, Julius, Ben and Adrian, who were the only guests left. When Kyle had yawned a couple of times. Julius commented if that was Kyle's way of telling them to leave, which he denied and told them they were welcome to stay. But he couldn't guarantee that he wouldn't fall asleep on Samuel's shoulder.

"Where are you staying, Adrian?" Kyle asked after everyone had decided to leave.

"At Julius and Ben's, where I stayed last night as well."

"You can stay here if you want," Samuel suggested. He was quite sure that Kyle and Adrian would want to spend some quality time with each other to catch up properly. He had only asked Adrian to stay with Ben and Julius the first night because he wanted Adrian's appearance to be a surprise for Kyle.

"Maybe not tonight, eh?" Adrian winked at them before pulling Kyle into a tight hug. He hesitated when it came to Samuel, but Samuel had no qualms about it and he pulled Adrian into a hug.

Kyle turned to Samuel when everyone was gone and smiled at him brightly as he went in for a kiss, leaving them both breathless when they finally parted. Then they made their way to the bedroom.

Samuel woke up to the feeling of Kyle's tongue playing with one of his barbells. When Samuel moaned softly, Kyle tugged on the barbell with his teeth, resulting in Samuel's moans becoming louder. Kyle used his hand to play with the other barbell, heightening Samuel's sensations. He loved how responsive he was when he heard Samuel moaning his name.

When Kyle could feel Samuel's hands gliding into his hair and then down to cup his jaw, Samuel gently trying to lift his head, Kyle flicked his tongue against the barbell one last time before letting go. He looked at Samuel with an angelic smile on his face and then leant in for a kiss, their tongues playfully fighting with each other.

Kyle lightly bit down on Samuel's bottom lip as they pulled apart and then admired the sight in front of him. Samuel's cheeks were flushed, but yet he still looked sleepy. Kyle counted himself lucky for being able to call Samuel his boyfriend.

"Okay?" Kyle asked as he gently stroked Samuel's face. When Samuel nodded his head, Kyle dived in for another kiss while straddling Samuel. He put his hands on Kyle's hips and then groaned into their kiss as he realized Kyle was naked.

Kyle pulled away and then kissed his way down to Samuel's chest, playing with his nipples a bit more before kissing his way even further down. When he reached the waistband of Samuel's boxers, he tugged them down, Samuel lifting his hips slightly to make it easier. Kyle grasped Samuel's half-hard cock firmly and gave it a few strokes, watching as he became fully hard as Samuel moaned softly. Kyle grabbed the condom he had left out earlier, and after opening it, rolled it down Samuel's length.

Just as Kyle was positioning himself so he could sink down on Samuel's cock, Samuel grabbed his hips tightly and he wouldn't let Kyle move. Kyle looked up concerned and confused. Samuel hadn't tensed up, yet he was shaking his head at Kyle and Kyle was wondering if he had overstepped his boundaries.

"You did nothing wrong," Samuel reassured as he saw the concerned frown on Kyle's face. "But we're not doing this without you being prepped."

Kyle smiled warmly at Samuel and then reached for one of his hands, which were still holding his hips tightly, and guided it to his entrance.

"I've opened myself up," Kyle grinned cheekily at Samuel as he saw Samuel's eyes getting darker at the thought of Kyle fingering himself open.

The grin was wiped off Kyle's face as Samuel thrust two fingers into him, hitting his prostate while Kyle groaned out loud.

Kyle couldn't take any more of the teasing and pushed Samuel's hand away. He took hold of Samuel's cock again and positioned it at his entrance, sinking down on it quickly as he moaned at the feeling of being filled. Samuel tried to give Kyle time to adjust, but Kyle started moving immediately, shifting until Samuel's cock hit his prostate with every thrust as Kyle was riding his cock frantically.

As Kyle leant down to kiss Samuel, Samuel could feel Kyle's pace slowing down. When they broke the kiss, Kyle was breathing heavily as he begged for harder and faster thrusts. Samuel flipped them over so he was lying on top and he resumed the pace Kyle had set while riding him. He sped up when Kyle pleaded with him again, grabbing his cock and stroking it in time with his thrusts. It didn't take long until Kyle shuddered in orgasm, Samuel following closely behind as he felt Kyle's muscles clenching around his cock.

"Fuck, you're amazing," Kyle whispered as Samuel nuzzled into his neck; both of them trying to get their breath back.

"So are you," Samuel shifted onto his side so he wasn't crushing Kyle and then reached out to trace the tattoo on Kyle's chest before his hand settled over Kyle's heart.

Two hours later, Kyle and Samuel were sat having lunch with Kyle's family at a small restaurant and Samuel still felt overwhelmed at how warmly Kyle's family had welcomed him when he first met them. He'd met Kyle's mum, Britt, and his stepfather and stepbrother first. Britt had made him feel so welcome, taking an immediate liking to him. Kyle's dad, James, and his family had been just as welcoming and Kyle's two little half-siblings had loved the attention they'd gotten from Kyle and Samuel.

Samuel was chatting away to Britt after lunch when Kyle appeared next to them, looking rather dissatisfied.

"Samuel Lowell!"

"What?" Samuel was confused. Kyle didn't sound pleased and he'd never used his full name before.

"Why was I just told that lunch has been paid for?"

"Oh that. Yeah, I invited you so I paid for it."

"You can't just pay for everyone's lunch. That's way too expensive!"

"You paid for everyone's lunch?" Britt was stunned and she put her hand on Samuel's arm. "Sweetie, Kyle is right. That is too much."

"It's fine. You can see it as my present…"

"Don't you dare tell me to see it as my birthday present from you! You already paid for Adrian's flight."

"Can we discuss this in private, Kyle?" Samuel asked quietly. He didn't like the attention that they'd drawn and he was starting to feel uncomfortable with Kyle raising his voice. "Kyle, Samuel is right; you should discuss this in private.

And preferably without you raising your voice," Britt interfered, she'd noticed Samuel tensing up when Kyle had raised his voice. He pulled his arm away from her hand.

Kyle bit his lip hard when he looked at Samuel. Now that he was looking at him properly he could clearly see how uncomfortable Samuel was and Kyle wanted to kick himself for causing this.

"I'm so sorry, Samuel," Kyle's voice was soft as he tried to hold back the tears that had formed in his eyes and he sat down next to Samuel. "Is it okay if I touch you?" Kyle wasn't sure if Samuel would want him to touch him. He feared he might have just jeopardized their relationship.

"Yes," was all Samuel could say before Kyle pulled him into a tight hug. Kyle was relieved that Samuel wasn't pushing him away. He placed soft kisses into Samuel's hair and onto his forehead while gently rubbing his back. Kyle was thankful when Samuel relaxed into him.

"Why don't you take Samuel home, sweetie?" Britt asked softly and Kyle just nodded his head.

Kyle had been quiet during the drive to Samuel's house, but Samuel didn't fail to notice that he was chewing on his lip the whole time. Samuel knew Kyle was worried. As much as he wanted to reassure Kyle that everything was okay, Samuel didn't think the car was the right place for it.

As soon as they were inside Samuel's house, Kyle turned to face Samuel and Samuel could see that the tears, which Kyle had been able to hold back at the restaurant, were flowing down his cheeks freely now.

"Have I ruined this?"

"Oh, Kyle, of course not. Come here," Samuel reached out and pulled Kyle into his arms, hugging him tightly as Kyle buried his face in Samuel's neck. "Shh, everything's okay, sweetheart," Samuel reassured while soothingly rubbing over Kyle's back and gently caressing the soft hair at the nape of his neck.

"I scared you," Kyle mumbled into Samuel's neck, his lips ghosting over Samuel's skin as he spoke.

"No, you really didn't."

Kyle pulled back and looked at Samuel in astonishment, studying his face intently. He could see that Samuel was telling the truth.

"But I made you uncomfortable. I'm really sorry about that, it was never my intention."

"Yes, you did, I can't deny that. But it's okay, you've realized it," Samuel gently cupped Kyle's face in his hands and wiped away the tearstains on Kyle's cheeks with his thumbs. "And even if you hadn't, I would have told you."

"Good. Alex is going to kill me for this, isn't he?"

Samuel chuckled softly, Kyle was probably right, but only if Alex ever found out about it. "He won't if you don't tell him. He won't hear it from me."

"Thanks. Samuel, can we talk about you paying for lunch?"

"Do we have to?"

"I promise I won't raise my voice again," Kyle reassured as he saw Samuel pulling a face.

"It's not that. I… Ugh okay, let's talk."

They got comfortable on the couch and Kyle grabbed Samuel's hand, gently caressing the back of it with his thumb as they looked at each other.

"You really didn't need to pay for everyone's lunch, Sam."

"It was no bother."

"But you already paid for Adrian's flight, in business class no less! He won't be able to pay you back, but I will."

"I don't want him to pay me back and neither do I want you to do it."

"You can't just spend so much money on me."

"Yes, I can. It's not like I don't have the money, I won't even notice that I spent that." Kyle looked stunned at Samuel. How could you not notice if you were spending that much money? Samuel smiled softly at Kyle's confused face as he brought his hand up and gently stroked the side of Kyle's face. "I'm sure you've noticed that I have money."

"Well, I guessed with where you live and the house you own, but it's none of my business."

Samuel just shrugged his shoulders; he didn't mind Kyle knowing that he was rich. "When I told you about my parents' accident, I didn't mention that I inherited a fortune. It really makes no difference how much I spend on a flight or if I pay for everyone's lunch."

"Are you that rich?"

"Yes. I wouldn't even have to work if I didn't want to, but I love my job."

Kyle nodded, chewing on his lip as he was deep in thought. "Okay, but just because you're rich, it doesn't mean that you have to spend a fortune on me. I don't want that, all I want is you."

Samuel smiled at Kyle, glad that he had judged him right, and he leant in, kissing Kyle softly. "You've got me," Samuel whispered as he broke the kiss and Kyle smiled back at him. "Although I can't promise not to spend money on you, but I'll try not to go overboard."

"Alright, I suppose that's all I can ask for."

Samuel laughed at the face Kyle pulled and then pulled him close, letting Kyle cuddle into him as he kissed his forehead. "Alex will love you for your attitude towards me being rich."

"Bad experiences?" Kyle asked as he squeezed Samuel's thigh.

"There were a few who tried. But Alex is a pretty good judge of character so he usually interfered. He told me he likes you because you didn't seem to be interested in me for just sex or money."

"I'd argue the sex part, I do enjoy that quite a lot," Kyle said as he pulled back, but when Samuel saw the devilish grin on his face, he knew Kyle was just teasing him. "But it's never been the main reason, only an added bonus."

"Yet you never made a move on our first date."

"And it was so hard not to! But I didn't want you thinking I only wanted sex."

"I'm sure you would have tried your luck at the wedding if that was all you were after. Who would say no to you anyway?"

"Not many," Kyle admitted. He knew he didn't have to work for it if he wanted a one-night stand.

"I wouldn't have said no either."

"On our first date?"

"Nor at the wedding." Kyle looked surprised at Samuel's admission. Samuel had told him that he'd had no interest in any more one-night stands and rather wanted a relationship. "Don't look so surprised, Kyle. You're fucking gorgeous," Samuel was telling the truth. He was done with one-night stands, but he would have made an exception for Kyle. Although he was sure he would have regretted it if they'd only ever had a one-night stand, not that he had to worry about that now.

Samuel suggested that they should spend the rest of the day with Adrian since he had come all the way to see Kyle. He also offered to let Adrian stay at his house, but Kyle declined, stating that it would be better if he stayed at Kyle's apartment. When Kyle saw the disappointment on Samuel's face, he reassured him that it would only be Adrian who was staying at Kyle's apartment. Kyle would stay with Samuel, if he was okay with that. The beautiful smile that appeared on Samuel's face was answer enough for Kyle. He leant in, letting his lips brush against Samuel's in a gentle kiss.

Chapter Ten

Christmas had come around a lot faster than either of them had anticipated and Samuel found himself being invited to spend it with Kyle and his whole family. When Samuel had told Alex he wasn't going to spend Christmas with him and his family like he did every year since his parents had passed away, Samuel apologized so many times. But Alex just told him to shut up and enjoy his Christmas with Kyle, glad to see him so happy.

It was Christmas Eve and they were watching Christmas movies, snuggled up together on the couch. They'd decided to stay up until midnight so they could exchange presents then, knowing that they wouldn't really have time to do that in peace the next day.

Samuel had been nervous ever since he decided on a present for Kyle. Now that it was only minutes away from midnight, it was getting so much worse. They'd been together for over six month now and Kyle more or less lived with him by now. Although, he still had his own apartment and Samuel had never officially asked him to move in. But he was going to change that.

Samuel was brought out of his thoughts as Kyle gently caressed the side of his face. When he looked at him, Kyle's bright blue eyes were gazing at him with concern.

"Are you okay? You're all fidgety."

"Yeah, I'm fine. Just a bit nervous."

"Why are you nervous?"

"Just not sure about your present."

"Aww, babe, I'm sure I'll love whatever it is," Samuel shrugged his shoulders as he licked his lips. He knew he didn't really have a reason to be nervous as he was quite sure that Kyle would be happy to move in with him. "Want to exchange presents now?"

When Samuel had agreed, both of them retrieved their presents and then met back in the living room. They sat down on the couch so they were facing each other.

"You go first," Samuel hoped that he would feel less nervous once he opened Kyle's present, or rather presents. There was one standing next to the couch and another one lying on his lap.

Kyle nodded and then grabbed the present that was standing next to the couch before handing it over to Samuel. He watched as Samuel carefully opened the paper and then gasped as he discovered a beautiful picture frame, which Kyle had built for him, with pictures of his parents and him with them.

"Kyle…" Samuel was lost for words as he looked at Kyle with tears in his eyes. Kyle reached out to gently squeeze his hand.

"Do you like it?"

"I love it. It's so beautiful."

"It always stuck in my mind that you said you couldn't find a picture frame you like to fit all of the pictures you wanted in so I decided to build one for you. I'm glad you like it."

"Thank you so much."

"You're welcome," Kyle grinned at Samuel before handing over the present that was lying on his lap.

"We said one present, Kyle." Samuel teased, but he took the present anyway.

"I know, but it's connected to the first one. So technically, it is one present."

Samuel laughed softly as he opened that present as well and revealed another picture frame that Kyle had made. This time it only contained one picture, which was a picture of Samuel and Kyle.

"Thank you, Kyle. I love them both." Samuel leant in and kissed Kyle softly before he pulled back again so he could hand him his present.

Kyle tore open the paper immediately and then lifted the lid of the little box to reveal a key ring with several keys on it.

"Move in with me?" Samuel asked when Kyle looked at him. He was still feeling a bit nervous, but when Kyle's face split into a huge grin he finally felt himself relax.

"Yes, I'd love to," Kyle breathed as he threw himself into Samuel's arms and showered his face with kisses.

"Stop it, Kyle," Samuel giggled when Kyle kept kissing his face. When he still didn't stop, Samuel brought his hands to Kyle's sides and started tickling him, effectively getting him to stop as he started laughing.

"No fair," Kyle pouted as he gently swatted Samuel's hands away. Samuel only smiled at Kyle as he brought one of his hands up and let his fingers glide through Kyle's soft hair, which he hadn't styled after his shower earlier.

"I love you," Samuel said as he gazed into Kyle's eyes.

"I love you." Kyle quickly kissed Samuel's nose before

he got up and switched off the TV. He then grabbed Samuel's hand and tugged on it until Samuel got up as well, following Kyle to the bedroom.

Just as Kyle had taken his jumper off, he felt Samuel's arms wrapping around his waist from behind, pressing their bodies together as Samuel kissed Kyle's shoulder. Kyle leant back into the embrace as Samuel kissed along his shoulder and then gently sucked on it. His hand found the bulge in Kyle's sweatpants, stroking his cock as Kyle moaned out loud.

Kyle tilted his head to the side to give Samuel better access to his neck and Samuel kissed his way to Kyle's ear before demanding, "Bed, now!"

"I love it when you're bossy," Kyle pulled out of the embrace and then let his sweatpants fall to the floor. He stepped out of them and then made his way over to the bed.

"No boxers?" Samuel raised an eyebrow as he got rid of his sweatpants and boxers before joining Kyle on the bed, making himself comfortable next to Kyle.

"What's the point? I knew they'd come off anyway," Kyle winked at Samuel while his hand was lazily stroking his cock, which Samuel slapped away gently.

"You cheeky little shit!" Kyle could hear the affection in Samuel's voice. He grinned at him before Samuel leant in to kiss him. Samuel pulled Kyle on top of him while they were kissing and then broke the kiss, grabbing the lube and a condom out of his bedside drawer. He pushed the lube into Kyle's hand as he said, "I want you to fuck me."

Kyle's eyes went black with lust. Samuel didn't ask to be fucked that often, but when he did, Kyle knew it was going to be incredible. He dived down to kiss Samuel and then kissed his way further down, playing with all of Samuel's piercings and teasing him while taking his time in opening him.

When Kyle decided that Samuel was open enough, after ignoring several pleas from him, he put on the condom and positioned the tip of his cock at Samuel's hole. He slowly pushed his way in until he bottomed out and then stilled, waiting for Samuel to adjust.

Kyle was mesmerized by how beautiful Samuel looked with his cheeks flushed and his head thrown back in pleasure. His tongue darted out to lick his lips as his hand reached out and took a hold of Kyle's, lacing their fingers together.

Kyle bit down on his lip hard when Samuel started rocking his hips. He felt so snug and warm around Kyle's cock that Kyle had to fight off his orgasm. Once Kyle was sure he wouldn't come straight away, he settled into a fast, steady rhythm while teasing Samuel's nipples as he played with his barbells.

Kyle knew he wouldn't be able to hold back much longer. He started tugging on Samuel's cock in the same pace as his thrusts while still teasing his nipples with his fingers. Whilst Kyle leant down to kiss Samuel, the angle changed and he hit Samuel's prostate, Samuel groaning into their kiss. Kyle knew it wouldn't take much more to make Samuel come so he broke their kiss and leant down to suck one of his nipples into his mouth. When Kyle gently bit down on the nub and then tugged on the barbell with his teeth, he could feel Samuel shudder in orgasm and clenching around his cock. This triggered Kyle's release as well who cried out in pleasure.

Samuel held him close while they were coming down from their high, not caring that Kyle was lying on top of him. Instead, he just reveled in their intimacy as Kyle placed soft kisses along his neck. Kyle eventually got Samuel to let him go and he rolled onto his side, cuddling into Samuel. His hands started roaming over Samuel's chest and abs.

"Really, Kyle?" Samuel asked incredulously as Kyle played with his barbells again. He was astonished that Kyle was up for another round already.

"Only if you're up for it."

"I don't think I'm up for it yet," Samuel winked at Kyle and then watched as a devilish grin appeared on his face.

"I'm sure I can change that."

"You are insatiable!"

"Only with you. So?"

"Alright, but first I have another present for you."

"We said one present, Sam," Kyle couldn't think of a better present than Samuel asking him to move in.

"Ah yeah, but that was not really a present. Come on, I'm sure you'll like that one too," Samuel nudged Kyle playfully and then he got up before holding his hand out to Kyle. Kyle looked at him confused but he did get up and took Samuel's hand, following him out of the bedroom. Samuel stopped in front of one of the guest rooms. "Go on, open the door."

Kyle opened the door and switched on the light, gasping in shock when he realized that the guest room had been transformed into an atelier. There were a lot of art supplies as well. He turned to look at Samuel when he felt his hand gently stroking over his back, but Kyle was still lost for words. He leant in and placed a quick kiss on Samuel's lips.

"This is awesome!" Kyle's smile was dazzling and Samuel was glad that he had decided to do this. He had gradually found out that Kyle liked sketching, drawing and painting, openly admiring how good he was at it. He wanted to make Kyle feel at home, knowing that Kyle would appreciate a place where he could sketch, draw or paint in piece if he wanted to. "Thank you, Samuel."

"I'm glad you like it," Samuel laughed as Kyle threw his arms around his neck and then yelped in surprise as Samuel lifted him off the ground, spinning them around.

Chapter Eleven

Samuel was sitting on the garden swing in Julius and Ben's garden, watching his friends play Frisbee when Alex joined him on the swing. They'd all been invited to celebrate Julius and Ben's third wedding anniversary. Since it was quite warm, they had decided to celebrate outdoors.

"I can't believe they've been married for three years already."

"You're one to talk. You and Mike have been married for over a year as well." Samuel smiled fondly at the memories of Alex and Mike's wedding. It had taken them long enough to finally take that step and Samuel was so happy for them when they finally did.

"So when are you making an honest man out of Kyle? I've got to return the favor of being best man, eh?" Alex's tone was teasing as he nudged Samuel. When he didn't get a response and he looked at Samuel, he could see a thoughtful expression on his face. "You want to marry him, don't you?"

"Don't you think it's too early?" Samuel bit down on his bottom lip as he waited for an answer from Alex. He didn't care about anyone else's opinion, but he did value Alex's opinion and he wanted to know what he thought.

"No, I don't. You might have only been together for just about three years, but you're perfect for each other, you love each other unconditionally." When Samuel didn't react, he continued, "Look at me, Samuel." Alex waited for Samuel to make eye contact before he carried on, "Forget what everyone else will think. Do you want to marry Kyle? Does it feel right for you?"

"Yes, I do want to marry him and it does feel right."

"Then what's stopping you?"

"Nothing," Samuel smiled at him mischievously.

"You've got this planned already, haven't you?" Alex laughed softly when Samuel confirmed it. "Tell me about it."

Samuel told him that he was originally planning to do it on the day of their third anniversary in two weeks. But he'd never get Kyle to leave the house long enough on that day so he could prepare everything. Kyle would also know something was up if Samuel invited him to a fancy restaurant, knowing that Samuel preferred spending time at home to going out. So he decided to do it the day before their anniversary. He'd spoken to Julius already and he was happy to help him out by keeping Kyle occupied until the early evening.

"Julius will send Kyle home when I've texted him that everything is ready."

"Have you got an engagement ring already?"

"I've looked around and I have a pretty good idea of what I want, but I'd like you to come along to help me decide."

"Of course, I'd love to. But you had better ask me to be your best man," Alex teased lightly.

"I will, there's no one else I'd rather have as my best man. Thanks, Alex."

"Anytime. You know I'd do anything for you, you're like a brother to me," Alex was surprised as Samuel pulled him into a tight hug.

"Same," was all Samuel murmured into Alex's neck before he placed a kiss on his cheek as he pulled back again.

"It's good to see you so happy, Samuel," Alex leant in and placed a quick, platonic kiss on Samuel's lips.

"Don't you have a husband you can kiss?" Kyle asked cheekily as he approached them.

"Nope, he was busy and Samuel wasn't," Alex winked at Kyle, who chuckled softly. He then took Samuel's outstretched hand, letting Samuel pull him closer and onto his lap. Kyle and Alex had fallen into an easy friendship and were always bantering with each other and teasing each other.

"Are you okay, babe?" Kyle asked as Samuel wrapped his arms around his waist and pulled him against his chest, turning his head slightly so he could see Samuel's face.

"Perfect," Samuel quickly kissed the side of Kyle's nose. He pressed a lingering kiss against his temple as well, Kyle smiling contently.

Alex always found it endearing that Kyle made sure Samuel was comfortable when there was a larger crowd of people around. Even when Samuel told him that he was fine, he would still come and check on him regularly.

"You're a good man, Kyle. You've been really great for Samuel." Kyle looked at Alex confused. He did get on great with Alex, but he'd never told him anything like that before. He wondered what had brought this on.

"Uh, thanks?" Kyle didn't mean for it to sound like a question, but he was still confused. "What's going on?"

"Nothing. Am I not allowed to pay you a compliment? It's just something I should have told you a lot sooner. I really appreciate you always being there for Samuel."

"That goes without saying, I love him." Kyle sighed contently when Samuel nuzzled into the back of his neck. He placed several kisses there, before pulling back and looking at Alex.

"Enough with the heavy, you sappy fool. I'm sure Kyle has known for a long time that you approve of him."

"Of course I have. The way you're interacting with me has always told me that, Alex."

"Good. You still deserved to hear it though," Alex smiled at them before pressing a kiss to each of their temples and then leaving them to find Mike.

Samuel was stood in the jewelers with Alex and he was admiring the perfect rings for Kyle and himself. When he had pointed the rings out to Alex, he had agreed straight away. Now, he was confused as to why Samuel wasn't asking to see the rings up close.

"Kyle is going to kill me if I buy them," Samuel whispered quietly, continuing when Alex only gave him a confused look, "Just look at the price."

"They're platinum; what do you expect? Besides it's not like you can't afford them."

"I have no problem spending that amount on the rings, but Kyle hates it when I spend that much on him."

"You know I really admire him for that, but that's just silly. Don't you think he'll turn a blind eye this time?"

"Kyle can be very stubborn. But I guess I'll find out. The rings are perfect and I'm sure he'll love them as well."

Samuel paid for the rings after looking at them closely and deciding on an inscription. He left the jewelers after being told that he could pick up the rings in two days.

Samuel was waiting for Kyle to come back from Julius and Ben's place. He'd sent Julius a text about half an hour ago that he had everything ready. He'd cooked one of Kyle's favorite meals and he'd also baked the cake that he had offered to Kyle on their first date, which Kyle still loved.

When he heard the front door closing, he made his way into the hall and watched as Kyle took his shoes off before turning around to face Samuel.

"Hey, are you okay?" Samuel was slightly alarmed as Kyle didn't look amused, but relaxed when Kyle gave him a genuine smile.

"Yes. I just don't know why Julius insisted I needed to come over and then kicked me out as soon as Ben got home. I could have spent the day with you instead," Kyle grumbled, which turned into a contented sigh when Samuel wrapped his arms around him and kissed his forehead tenderly.

"You can spend the evening with me. I've cooked dinner and we can relax on the couch afterwards if you want."

"Sounds great," Kyle beamed at Samuel and then leant in to kiss him.

Once they were finished with dinner, they made themselves comfortable on the couch. Kyle snuggled into Samuel's side as Samuel put his arm around Kyle's shoulder, pulling him close.

"I love you, Kyle. And I'm so glad that we got to meet each other at Ben and Julius' wedding. I couldn't imagine my life without you and I can't wait to spend forever with you."

"I love you too, Samuel. And I can't wait to spend the rest of my life with you either," Kyle said after he pulled back and then leant forward, kissing Samuel deeply.

"Would you like some dessert?" Samuel asked when they'd broken the kiss. He knew Kyle never said no to dessert. "I've made a cake as well."

"Yes, please, I love your cakes."

Samuel kissed the tip of Kyle's nose before he untangled himself and went off to get the cake, returning with it shortly.

"Aren't you going to have some cake as well?" Kyle frowned when he saw that Samuel was only carrying one plate.

"Not going to share with me?" Samuel pouted. He didn't give Kyle a chance to reply as he sat down and handed the plate over to Kyle. "There you go then."

Kyle was just about to reassure Samuel that he would indeed share with him when he looked at the cake and was left speechless. The cake was a miniature version of the cake that Kyle had been offered on their first date. This time, there was something written on the icing. The letters were bright blue and read 'Marry Me?'

Kyle gasped in surprise, and when he looked at Samuel. He was holding out a little box with an engagement ring in it.

"Yes!" Kyle breathed and then put the cake down on the coffee table before throwing himself into Samuel's arms and kissing him passionately.

When they finally stopped kissing, Samuel held out the ring box to Kyle, who took out the ring and admired it closely.

"Do I even want to know how much this cost?"

"Kyle," Samuel groaned. He had really hoped that Kyle wouldn't argue about how much it cost. "Please don't do this."

"Okay."

"No arguing that the ring is too expensive?" Samuel was surprised, although he wasn't sure if he should believe it yet.

"Well, it probably is, but no, I won't argue. It's so beautiful and I love it! But…" Samuel groaned at the word, he knew it was too good to be true. "Shh, let me finish. I'd like us to make a compromise."

"Go on," Samuel encouraged even though he wasn't sure he wanted to know and his expression remained skeptical.

"We're not going to buy wedding rings. I want this ring as my wedding ring."

"Okay, as long as I'm allowed to add something to it."

"I guess that's only fair," Kyle held out the ring to Samuel, who just looked at him confused. "Put it on," He said as he held his hand out as well and Samuel took the ring before sliding it onto Kyle's finger.

"I love you, Kyle, so much."

"I love you too. Did you get a ring for yourself as well?" Kyle asked excitedly, and when Samuel nodded, he told him to get it because he wanted to put it on Samuel's finger as well. Kyle smiled widely when he saw that the ring was identical to his. The only difference was the inscription, and he gently took Samuel's hand in his, sliding the ring onto his finger.

Kyle had just returned from an afternoon he'd spent with Julius and he was looking for Samuel, who he eventually found working out in the gym. Kyle stood in the doorway watching as Samuel, who had his back turned to the door, was lifting weights. He admired the way Samuel's muscles rippled with every lift.

"Hey," Samuel's voice was soft and breathless as he stopped lifting. He looked at Kyle's reflection in the mirror before making his way over to him, placing a quick kiss on his lips. "I've only started my workout; I didn't think you'd be back so early."

"That's okay. I'm sure I can entertain myself," Kyle winked at Samuel with a cheeky smile on his lips.

"I'm sure you can. Will you put dinner into the oven in a while? I've prepared a casserole, it just needs to go into the oven for about half an hour."

"Of course, I will," Kyle leant in to kiss Samuel softly before he left him to finish his workout.

It was over an hour later when Samuel had finished his workout and he made his way upstairs to take a shower. When he reached the ground floor and didn't get a smell of the casserole cooking in the oven, he knew Kyle had forgotten about it. He knew exactly where he would find him. Samuel put the casserole into the oven and set the timer on it before he made his way upstairs to take a shower.

Once Samuel was finished with his shower and dressed in some comfy clothes, he made his way to Kyle's atelier, smiling when he discovered he was right. He leant against the doorframe and watched Kyle painting. Kyle was always so relaxed when he was painting or drawing. He usually zoned out completely, forgetting everything else around him. So it came as no surprise that he hadn't heard Samuel entering the room.

"Dinner will be ready in twenty minutes," Samuel's voice was soft as he spoke. He didn't want to give Kyle a fright, although he had waited until Kyle dipped the brush into one of the color pots before he spoke, not wanting him to ruin the picture he was working on.

"Oh shit, I completely forgot about that," Kyle gave Samuel a sheepish look as he turned to face him.

"I've noticed, but I'm not surprised," Samuel chuckled softly as he stepped closer to Kyle and then studied the picture he was painting. "Is that the picture of Alex's parents?"

"Yes. What do you think?"

"It looks amazing so far. I'm sure Alex and his parents will love it," Samuel wrapped his arm around Kyle and then pulled him into his side, kissing his temple gently. Alex had asked him if Kyle would paint a picture of his parents for their wedding anniversary, which Kyle had agreed to, although he didn't usually paint for others.

"Thanks, babe. But I know why I don't paint for others; it's too stressful to work with a deadline."

"You've got more than enough time to finish it and you're almost done anyway, so there's no need for you to worry."

"Yeah, it shouldn't take me much longer to finish it," Kyle turned his head to look at Samuel, smiling as he placed a kiss on his cheek. "But now let's go have dinner."

When they'd finished dinner they settled down on the couch, watching TV as Samuel absentmindedly ran his fingers through Kyle's hair. Kyle was tugged into his side with his head lying on Samuel's shoulder. After a while, Kyle lifted his head and placed a kiss on Samuel's jaw, his hand squeezing his thigh.

"What are you thinking about?"

"Would you allow me to arrange our honeymoon? I want it to be a surprise for you," Samuel turned his head to look at Kyle so he could judge his reaction.

"Samuel," Kyle groaned as he sat up properly, but he was still facing Samuel. He knew when Samuel said he wanted to arrange it, it meant he wanted to pay for it. "You're already paying for our wedding, at least let me pay for our honeymoon."

"Please?" Samuel begged as he looked at Kyle with a pouty face.

"You've got this planned already, haven't you?" Kyle sighed as Samuel nodded his head before he continued, "I don't want you to spend so much money on me. I just feel like I'm using you."

"Kyle, you're not. Not once have you asked me to pay for anything since I've known you. On the contrary, you normally argue against me paying for stuff."

"And lose the argument half the time. I thought I was stubborn, but you can be pretty stubborn as well. But others don't see it that way, they don't know that I don't want you to pay all the time."

Samuel reached out and ran his fingers through Kyle's hair, his hand eventually moving down to cradle Kyle's cheek while his thumb gently caressed it.

"Has anyone said anything to you?" Kyle shook his head carefully, not wanting Samuel to take his hand away, before he nuzzled into Samuel's hand and he placed a kiss on the inside of his wrist. No one had said anything, but Kyle wasn't stupid. There was bound to be people who thought he was only in it for the money. "Then don't let anyone else's opinion matter, it's none of their business. All that matters is us. I just want our wedding and honeymoon to be special, sweetheart."

"Okay," Kyle finally gave in as he realized Samuel was right. It was no one else's business.

"Really?"

"Yes. But just to make this clear, you're never spending so much money on me ever again. The wedding and the honeymoon will be the only exceptions."

"I promise. Thank you, Kyle," Samuel smiled happily as he leant in and kissed Kyle softly.

Chapter Twelve

It was a year after the proposal. Alex stood watching Samuel as he got dressed for the wedding and he was surprised at how calm Samuel seemed to be. It had been a challenge to convince Samuel and Kyle not to spend the night before the wedding together. But Alex and Julius had managed it in the end.

"Are you nervous?"

Samuel looked at Alex and smiled softly. "No. Should I be?"

"Not afraid Kyle will say no or not turn up?"

Samuel laughed out loud at that, these ideas were just ridiculous to him. "Nope. If Kyle wouldn't want this, he would have said no when I proposed. The first thing Ben told me about Kyle was that you couldn't make him do anything he didn't want to do and it's so very true."

"That's good. I was nervous when I married Mike."

"I know, I was there! But it took you ages to get married in the first place. Not that you had anything to be worried about," Samuel winked at him as he put on his suit jacket. "Are you ready to go?"

"Shouldn't I be asking you that? But you seem very eager to go." Alex laughed as he stepped closer to Samuel and pulled him into a tight hug. "I'm so happy that Kyle is the right one for you."

"I can't wait to finally marry him. And I'm extremely happy about it as well. Now come on, I don't want to make him wait."

"And have him think you're standing him up?" Alex winked at Samuel and then laughed when Samuel slapped his arm lightly.

"Kyle knows me, he won't think that."

The wedding was beautiful with just family and close friends present. Everyone could feel the happiness radiating from Kyle and Samuel as they made their rounds so that they'd spent at least a little time with each of their guests.

Kyle and Samuel were wrapped up in each other's arms while dancing to a slow song until Kyle pulled back a bit so he could look at Samuel.

"Are you finally going to tell me where we're going for our honeymoon?" Kyle had been curious to find out for a while. But Samuel hadn't given anything away so far and Kyle had eventually stopped asking.

"Hm, I don't know," Samuel laughed as Kyle looked at him with big blue eyes and an adorable pout on his lips, which he kissed off quickly. "Alright, alright. We're going to Aitutaki, it's one of the Cook Islands. I've rented a honeymoon villa on a private isle called Akitua Private Island."

"Samuel…" Kyle was left speechless. He hadn't expected Samuel to rent them a villa on a private island. "Wow. Isn't Aitutaki known as Honeymoon Island?"

"Yes, it is. I see you've done some research," Samuel grinned when he realized Kyle must have looked up some places.

"I might have checked out some honeymoon destinations since you didn't give anything away. It's meant to be really beautiful with a lagoon surrounding it. I can't wait to go and explore it. Thank you. I love you, hubby," Kyle beamed at Samuel before kissing him softly.

"I love you too, my husband," Samuel whispered as they pulled apart.

When Kyle and Samuel had gotten home, Samuel had pinned Kyle against the closed door and kissed him passionately while unbuttoning Kyle's waistcoat. They had both agreed before the wedding that neither of them wanted to get drunk as they wanted to be able to remember the whole wedding—including the wedding night. Kyle had also insisted that they'd spend their wedding night in their own home and their own bed, knowing Samuel would be most comfortable at home.

Kyle broke the kiss when Samuel had succeeded in unbuttoning his waistcoat. Both of them panted heavily as they gazed at each other with lust-filled eyes. He grabbed Samuel's hand and pulled him upstairs to their bedroom. Samuel drew him close again as he went in for another kiss.

When Samuel pushed the waistcoat of Kyle's shoulder, Kyle broke the kiss again, insisting that they both get undressed before continuing. He didn't want to risk ruining their wedding suits in the heat of the moment. Both of them stripped out of their suits while watching the other do so. Samuel grabbed the lube out of the nightstand and then left it on top of the chest of drawers.

Samuel turned to Kyle again and pulled him flush against himself as he kissed him one more time, letting his hands roam over Kyle's back. When Kyle wrapped his arms around Samuel's neck, Samuel lifted him off the ground. Kyle wrapped his legs around his waist automatically, knowing that Samuel was easily able to take his weight.

Samuel pressed Kyle against the wall as he broke their kiss so he could leave a trail of kisses along Kyle's neck while Kyle reached for the lube. As soon as Samuel heard the click of Kyle opening the tube, he pulled back and then held up his hand. Kyle understood the hint and squeezed some lube onto Samuel's fingers before Samuel reached around and slowly, teasingly, circled Kyle's hole with his finger. When Kyle started to squirm slightly, Samuel pushed one finger in and sought out Kyle's prostate, Kyle moaning in pleasure when he found it. It didn't take long until Samuel slid a second finger in and gently opened Kyle up, grazing his prostate occasionally.

"Stop teasing me. I want you."

"Patience, love," Samuel whispered into Kyle's ear as he nudged Kyle's prostate one last time before withdrawing his fingers. He grabbed the lube and handed it to Kyle before making sure he had a secure grip on Kyle. Kyle took his arms away from around his neck so he could coat Samuel's cock with lube while stroking him a couple of times. Kyle guided Samuel's cock to his entrance, Samuel pushing in gently, yet steadily, as Kyle wrapped his arms around his neck once again and then started to rock his hips as soon as Samuel was fully inside.

Samuel settled into a rhythm easily, knowing exactly what both of them needed now. He changed the angle of his thrusts until Kyle cried out in pleasure, telling Samuel that he was hitting his prostate with every thrust now.

"Stroke yourself, Kyle. I don't want to let go of you," Samuel said as he picked up his pace while leaning in to kiss Kyle. Kyle made no move to stroke himself, but he brought one of his hands to Samuel's chest, pinching his nipples and tugging on his barbells, Samuel groaning into their kiss. When he knew Samuel was close enough to his release, he finally wrapped his hand around his own cock and gave it a few rough strokes which matched Samuel's pace. It wasn't long before he came with a gasp of Samuel's name, his muscles clenching around Samuel's cock as his come was spurting over his hand and Samuel's abs. This triggered Samuel's release, who came with a quiet moan as he buried his face into Kyle's neck.

Kyle stroked over Samuel's back and through his hair soothingly, both of them breathing heavily as they tried to get their breaths back. When Samuel showed no sign of moving, Kyle placed a soft kiss into his hair and then whispered, "Put me down, babe."

"Yeah, give me a second."

Kyle was surprised when Samuel moved immediately. Instead of putting him down, Samuel carried him to the bed and gently set him down there, placing a kiss on the tip of Kyle's nose. Kyle grabbed Samuel's hand when he made to move away and pulled him down onto the bed next to him, pushing him down on his back.

"Go get comfy, I'll get a wet cloth," Kyle said as he gently patted Samuel's thigh and then went to the bathroom to clean himself up before returning to Samuel to wipe his abs clean as well.

They'd been lying on the bed in companionable silence for a while. Kyle was cuddled into Samuel's side with his face buried into the side of Samuel's neck, placing soft, little kisses there occasionally. But he pulled back eventually and propped himself up on his elbow as he looked at Samuel. Samuel turned his head to look at him as well.

"Thank you."

"What for?" Samuel turned onto his side as he reached out and gently stroked the side of Kyle's face.

"For loving me. Our wedding has been absolutely amazing and I have no doubt that our honeymoon will be too."

"Always and forever. Thank you for loving me, too."

Kyle smiled adoringly at Samuel before he leant in, capturing Samuel's lips in a passionate kiss. He pushed him onto his back and straddled him, letting his hands roam over his chest.

"Are you up for another round, babe?" Kyle asked breathlessly when they broke apart, a cheeky smile on his lips. He rocked his hips against Samuel's, rubbing their half-hard cocks together. Samuel moaned softly as he let his hands slide down over Kyle's back to his ass, squeezing his cheeks tightly.

"Still so insatiable."

"Only for you. And you love it."

"Yes, I do. And I love you."

"Love you too."

www.ingramcontent.com/pod-product-compliance
Lightning Source LLC
Chambersburg PA
CBHW031033190726
48286CB00003BA/1145